Legacy of an Alask

Right Place

Copyright 2021 by Jocelyn Ludwigsen. All Rights Reserved.

No part of this document may be reproduced or transmitted in any form or by any means, electronic, mechanical, photocopying, recording or otherwise without the prior written permission of Jocelyn Ludwigsen or her designated representative.

All rights of distribution, including film, radio and television, photomechanical reproduction, sound carriers of any kind, reprints or reprints in accumulation and recovery in data processing systems of all kinds are reserved.

Photographs and documents are the property of Jocelyn Ludwigsen.

ACKNOWLGEMENTS:

I would like to thank the many people who helped me put this book together without which this would not be possible:

Dave Kiffer, who penned this book and spent many hours traveling to interview me and listen to my life story.

Jocelyn, my daughter, and her husband Herb for finding, editing, and choosing the pictures and documents presented and to Robinlyn Holmes for additional editing.

Collen Prewett, Graphic Designer, who generously donated his time and talent creating the front cover.

Last my darling wife Ann who help me remember the finer details of my experiences and in general puts up with me.

Herman Ludwigsen

Contents

Authors Note 6

Eagle Eye 7

Fearless Parents and North to Alaska 11

World War II 18

Fishing and Fish Pirating in the 1940s 20

Basketball 21

The Don Carlos 22

Always Looking to Fly 27

Saved by the Military and One Beautiful Girl 30

After the Army, Back to Ketchikan 33

Bethel Charter Service 42

Time to Head Home 55

Otters and Transponders 63

Humanity 67

Hung Up His Wings 75

Beating the Odds 76

Herman, FAA, and the Wright Brothers 80

Aviation timeline provided by the FAA 82

Trapper/Hunter 83

The Planes 96

    Grumman Goose 96

    DeHavilland Beaver 98

Cessna's 100

    Piper Super Cub 102

    Pilatus Porter 103

    Curtiss C-46 103

The Right Place at the Right Time

Herman Ludwigsen's half century as a legendary bush pilot, Alaskan fisherman, hunter, and trapper

Authors Note

Often you hear of a historical figure who was born "ahead of their time." Sometimes, someone living in the present will say 'they wish they had been born in an earlier time when life was different'. For nearly a century, Herman Ludwigsen has been in exactly the right place at the right time. Specifically, he has had an uncanny knack for locating downed planes and their passengers, rescuing, or recovering dozens of people from the Alaska wilderness. A skill he attributes to "flying low" to the ground, but also to being in the air at the right time to spot something, maybe even just an unusual glimmer in the endless forest or the snow-covered tundra. In a general sense, Ludwigsen has also lived in a time when he could do just what he wanted as far as flying and living the outdoor life. Had he been born a couple of decades earlier; he would not have been around for the heyday of the Alaskan Air Taxi industry. Had he been born later; he would have been in an outdoors world that was much more heavily regulated – and limited – than it was in the middle of the 20th Century. In the words of his wife Ann, "Herman did exactly everything he ever wanted to do with his life." This book is the story of Herman Ludwigsen and his wife Ann, but it is also the story of Alaska, at a time when someone like Ludwigsen could truly make his life what he wanted. With a little bit of luck, a fair amount of guts and unsurpassed skill, Ludwigsen survived more than half a century in an industry not known for its longevity; where every day the weather could literally kill you. He also commercially fished, hunted, and trapped - he even spent time as a 'fish pirate', an equally legendary occupation in the fish-trap era of Alaska, prior to Statehood in 1959. And unlike a lot of pilots, he also recognized, in his 70s, when it was time to hang it up, to enjoy the long retirement he had undoubtedly earned. Clearly, Herman Ludwigsen has lived – very well – at just the right time.

Dave Kiffer
Ketchikan, Alaska
December 2020

Eagle Eye

From several hundred feet in the air, a great deal of Southeast Alaska looks pretty much the same.

Seemingly endless stretches of fjords, inlets, and straits, punctuated with islands covered by America's largest temperate rainforest. The tree covering is so dense that it is usually impossible to see the ground, and, after a while, all the islands start to blend together into a relentless patchwork. Only the most practiced eyes can tell them apart.

Or notice something that is out of the ordinary.

But after countless hours spent in the air over Southeast Alaska, and more spent traveling the waters on fishing boats, Herman Ludwigsen had just such a pair of practiced-eyes and when he spotted something unusual on a hillside in Boca de Quadra in August of 1953, he knew he had found what he - and every pilot in the area - was looking for.

Most Ketchikan-area residents are familiar with the plane crash of legendary pilot Harold Gillam in Boca de Quadra back in 1943. But almost exactly a decade later there was another crash in Boca de Quadra, barely a mile away from where Gillam's plane went down.

This one involved Ellis Hall, the multimillionaire owner of Texas-based Condor Petroleum. Hall was on a vacation with his wife, two daughters and a family friend in Southeast Alaska. After visiting Juneau, Ellis was piloting his de Havilland DH 104 Dove, a large twin-engine plane. The plane would disappear after leaving Annette Island on August 17, 1953 leading to a month-long search, before the wreckage was found by Ketchikan pilot Ludwigsen.

Hall had landed his plane at Annette because the weather was beginning to deteriorate but he was determined to press on to his next stop, in Smithers, British Columbia on the way home to New Mexico.

"He knew that Ellis Air was not flying as the winds were 80-90 mph," Ludwigsen said recently. "He decided to leave anyway. He did not make it."

When Hall was reported missing it created one of the biggest searches in Southeast Alaska history.

"What happened was, it was pretty (bad) weather and they picked up ice and then the turbulence became bad, and they tried to go back (to Annette) but the ice and the heavy turbulence impacted the airplane and it fell apart in the air," Ludwigsen said.

When the plane was finally found, not far from where Gillam's plan had gone down a decade before, the debris was spread over a large area, so it was clear the plane came apart in the air rather than when it hit the ground.

"Everyone in town was searching for 30 days," Ludwigsen said. "All the gas was free from Condor Petroleum. They had wanted nine planes searching. The Canadian and US Coast Guard were involved and after they stopped searching, Condor still wanted the little guys to continue. (Hall) was the owner of a big company so lawyers wanted finality."

Condor Petroleum also offered a $25,000 reward for whomever found the plane. After a couple of weeks, it was increased to $30,000.

The search covered an area 50 miles north of Ketchikan to Prince Rupert and 90 miles to the south. For the first two weeks, the disappearance and search were national news, stories from Ketchikan appeared in newspapers from coast to coast.

An example was an Associated Press story that appeared in dozens of papers three days after the crash.

The AP story noted that searchers were now directing their attention 30 miles north of Ketchikan because two loggers at a camp on the northern end of Revillagigedo Island had seen a ball of fire on a nearby mountainside.

"A fish trap tender, operating about five miles from the logging camp, told of hearing a plane's engines Monday evening that suddenly died out," the Associated Press added. "A searching plane saw two clipped trees which might have been sheared off by a crippled plane before crashing."

Ludwigsen said that eventually the other pilots had to break off the search, but because Ludwigsen was only working part time he continued searching during his off hours. Poking into the valleys and channels near Boca de Quadra with his Piper Super Cruiser. He said that he and other local pilots made a pact that if any of them found the Hall plane, they would split the $30,000 reward with the others.

One day, after telling his wife Ann he was going duck hunting, he flew back down to Boca de Quadra and got lucky.

"I flew down and looked at the left side of Quadra at Porpoise Point, I was flying so close that I could see between the trees and that's when I saw something white laying on the ground. There had been lots of rain, so the creeks were foaming white, but this was not foam. It was not moving it just lying there between the big spruce trees. I circled back to the north looking up the five-mile valley for parts of the plane. As I made a turn, I saw a green wing on the mountainside. I could see the circular part of the wing structure; I knew then it was plane parts."

It was also clear that none of the five people on board the plane had survived the crash.

Ludwigsen contacted Webber Air in Ketchikan and determined that what he saw was not part of the Gillam plane which had been intact when it crashed less than a mile away from where he spotted the Hall wreckage. Ludwigsen continued to circle around and spotted more wreckage in the nearby valley.

"I flew back to Ketchikan and Bruce Johnstone and I were the first back to the shore," he said. "We walked up the mountain. The bodies had been there over a month and the animals and insects had taken their toll. (The passenger's) watches were stopped by the impact and a five-carat diamond ring glistened on one of the fingers."

The Coast Guard recovered the bodies, but most of the plane debris was left on site, just as had been done with the Gillam flight. Ludwigsen got his check for $30,000 (more than $280,000 today).

Ludwigsen said he donated $5,000 of the money to local charities and gave $1,000 to his brother Harry to build baseball dugouts at Walker Field, where Harry was a coach and longtime volunteer. Ludwigsen bought his wife a new washer and dryer and some other household goods and he paid for his mother to fly to Chicago to visit a brother she hadn't seen in over 30 years.

"I invited all the other pilots and their wives to a dinner at the Narrows Restaurant," Ludwigsen said. "The pilots each had a $1,000 check under their plates."

Meanwhile, Ellis Hall's surviving children inherited some $24 million ($231 million today) in Condor Petroleum stock. One of his sons, James Ellis Hall, would go on to found Chaparral Motors, partner with Carroll Shelby, and become one of the world's premier race car designers.

Ludwigsen would go on to a five-decade career in local aviation and was involved in numerous other searches. In 2016, one of Hall's granddaughters visited Ketchikan on a cruise ship to specifically thank Ludwigsen for finding the plane and helping recover the bodies.

Frequently changing weather and challenging schedules - particularly during the more active summer seasons - means that pilots need to balance caution with "making money" by being in the air. Those that don't find the narrow line between the two don't often survive. Commercial air taxi operations are one of the most dangerous occupations in Alaska.

In Alaska, they say there are bold bush pilots and old bush pilots, but no old and bold bush pilots.

Yet, there is an exception to the rule, Ludwigsen, a pilot who was known for sometimes pushing the envelope and flew for more than half a century in the most challenging conditions in both Southeast and Southwest Alaska, is the exception to the rule.

He put in more than 32,000 flight hours in a variety of planes, ranging from Piper Super Cubs - sneaking in and out of tiny mountain lakes, to large twin engine C46 cargo planes - delivering tons of supplies to the North Slope to help build the Cold-War era Distant Early Warning system.

Along the way, Ludwigsen - who came to Alaska with his family during the Great Depression - also became a commercial fisherman, a prominent hunter and trapper and even a fish pirate, in the days before Alaska statehood, when salmon traps dominated - and threatened to wipe out Alaska's salmon industry. This is his story.

Fearless Parents and North to Alaska

Herman Nels Ludwigsen was born on November 20, 1927 in Seattle, Washington, the eighth and last child of Nels Christian Ludwigsen, a German immigrant from Hamburg, who was born on the Danish island of Sylt.

Nels Ludwigsen was a ship carpenter who had joined the German Navy and sailed around the world before ending up in South

America, just before World War I broke out. Nels was in Valpariso, Chile when he had a premonition about the war began, and he asked the captain if he could jump ship and the captain said yes. He eventually made his way to Astoria Oregon where he had relatives.

Amalie Smerratt met Nels at a dance social. During their two-year courtship Nels was at sea with the German Imperial Navy. It was at this time that Nels jumped ship and headed to Oregon. She got a letter from Nels asking her to join him. Amalie, born in northern Germany, was 23 years old when she decided to find Nels and marry him. She saved her money and sold her diamond earrings and mother's wedding ring to buy a ticket on one of the last ships leaving for America before World War I. Upon landing in New York despite knowing no English, she made her way by rail to Chicago, Illinois where she had relatives. She continued her cross-country train journey and met up with and learned Nels was in Salem, Oregon and took a train there to find him. She found Nels and shortly after and married on Sept 6, 1914 in Astoria, Oregon.

Nels and Amalie had five sons: Harry, Arnold, Peter, Alfred, and Herman and three daughters, Cora, Inez and Helen.

The family lived on a houseboat, in Seattle, near the Ballard Locks.

"It was in Seattle that I fell in love for the first time," Herman said. "I was six or seven years old. I had to walk down past the apple trees on Commodore Way to see her. She was a grand old lady. You could see that she had good structure and fine lines, a little dusty maybe but that did not affect my feelings for her. She was a 1930s biplane with a wooden prop and the Chinese family who owned it did not mind my visiting her."

Ludwigsen said he also enjoyed watching the biplanes and triplanes flying over Lake Washington.

When Herman was 9, Nels Ludwigsen decided to move the family to Alaska where the job prospects were better.

"Dad got tired of Seattle," Ludwigsen said. "We were dead poor; we were practically in the bread line."

Nels Ludwigsen, an accomplished boat builder, built a 36-foot trolling boat, to transport the 10 Ludwigsen's north. The "Amalie" was a double-ender, that – at the time – was much larger than most of the trollers in the local fleet. In those days, most of the trollers were in the 28–32foot range. Once the boat was finished Ludwigsen got his friend "Tonto" Bill to help him and his family sail up north.

"Bill had talked to my Dad many times about coming up north fishing with him but instead ended up guiding us with two other boats." Our destination was Sitka.

Ludwigsen doesn't remember how long it took to travel from Seattle to Ketchikan, but since the boat's top speed was only about 7 to 8 knots, it would have taken at least two weeks for the family to travel the approximately 650 miles. Ludwigsen does remember stopping in Bellingham and Bella Bella and other places along the way, usually to get additional fuel and supplies.

"We were all seasick," he said. "It was tough."

The family arrived in Ketchikan in the spring of 1938. Nels decided Sitka was too far and stayed in Ketchikan. Initially, they lived aboard the boat and eventually found a place on the water side of Tongass Avenue.

"We were glad to be off the boat, but the house was a ratty old one" he said. "The bathroom had a hole in the floor, and you could see the beach below. Then we started to build a boat shed, near 1500 Tongass Avenue. It had marine slipways to launch boats. (Dad) built two big boats there and rebuilt a lot of boats for places like Hydaburg and the "stink plant" - a waste reduction plant in Ward Cove. They had the "Falcon" and another (boat) that my Dad rebuilt."

Ludwigsen also remembers when the Golden Rhine Brewery and the Columbia Cleaners were across the street, as was Edwards Wire Rope company.

"This big German guy owned the Golden Rhine Brewery. He saw that I was a young, scrawny punk so he gave me a whole bunch of free beer tickets to take down to the Alaska Steamship Dock and give them to everybody," Ludwigsen said "I can remember that really well. I remember walking into the brewery, and it smelled awfully good."

Ludwigsen also remembers selling newspapers as a young boy.

"I used to stand there by Race Drug and shout "Fisherman's News, Fisherman's News," he said. He also sold the competing paper, the Ketchikan Chronicle.

"I wanted to work and soon had saved enough for a Sears Hawthorne bike," he said. "It was a red thing with stripes."

He also earned money working at the Ketchikan Cold Storage.

"Some of the old guys were too tired to unload their halibut boats," he said. "I would sling loads of halibut and clean up bin boards for them. I used to shovel herring on the "Rio Grande", Francis Murphy's boat, and the "Pirate ", Andy Gunderson's boat. They gave me nickels and dimes for my help. I was never without nickels and dimes."

He also did other tasks at the cold storage building, which was located near where the Ketchikan tunnel is now. When there were no boats to unload, Ludwigsen would either make wooden boxes in the dry room or glaze fish in the freezer room.

"I would go into the freezer compartment that was 30-40 degrees below zero," he recalls. "Two guys would go in together and the door would slam shut. There were no phones, just a big latch with a big knob that would release the outer latch. Once someone was inside a red light came on outside to let people know there were folks working inside. There were piles of halibut and salmon in there, plus a tank of water. I would put fish on a table, hook them on a cable and lower them into the water a couple of times to ice glaze them. Then I put the fish on a cart and took them to the corner that was set aside for the company that owned the fish. Sometimes only one or two halibut would fit on the two wheeled carts. Next, I would bring in a hose and spray them down. It put a milky white layer of ice on the fish. The room was stacked to the ceiling with halibut."

His mother was not enthused when he came home from a day at the cold storage.

"My Mom would hold her nose because I stunk so bad," he said. "The bathroom and the bathtub weren't in the house. We had to go into a shed. She would run the water in the bathtub and pour in Lysol to get the stink off me!"

He was also a part-time "soda jerk" at Federal Drug store on Mission Street in downtown Ketchikan.

While attending nearby White Cliff Elementary School, Ludwigsen was "schooled" by watching the early pilots of the day, such as Bob Ellis and Herb Munter, come and go from docks near the family home.

Ketchikan in the 1930s and 40s was a special place, Ludwigsen said.

"Like on the Fourth of July when everyone would head to Black Sands Beach on Gravina Island,". "The canneries would all shut down and we would all get on the barges and fish scows. That was the Eagles picnic. They would furnish hot dogs, pop, hell everything was free! Big time! Lots of people, lots of fun. We had foot races and swimming races and horseshoes; nobody was in a hurry. It was just a laid-back type of event and everybody had a few beers." Ludwigsen said that in town Dock Street was closed on the Fourth.

"They had a big sawdust pile for the kids to find money by digging around in it!" he said. "There were boxing matches at the ballpark. In the water there were seine boat races, and tugboat tug of wars, trolling boat races and logrolling contests. Everybody was seeing if they could beat each other."

Ludwigsen said that winters were also special times, if you were a kid in the First City.

"They'd shut down Main Street for sliding in the snow," he said. "We'd start way up the hill by the Revilla Apartments. Sleds, toboggans, and all. Hell, everybody was sledding down that sucker! Then you'd end up clear down at the Spruce Mill by Bucey's garage. That was a lot of fun. That was back when we had winters in Ketchikan. The ice froze clear across the bay. In the channel it was not thick enough to walk on, we had to have boats go out and break it up."

He said the ice was thick enough to skate on Thomas Basin and also on the area lakes.

"We would row across the bay at night in the moonlight and go over to Long Lake," he said. "That's when people always lived over on Gravina. There were always big parties there on the ice!"

Gravina was also an important location for some of Ludwigsen's first hunts.

"I would go deer hunting by rowing across the Tongass Narrows to Gravina in a double-ended rowboat," he said. "I would shoot a deer, clean it and row back to Ketchikan. I stored the deer in a locker at the cold storage building. The locker always smelled like ammonia. There was a tunnel attached to the same building. Erickson had a meat market that had beautiful meat, but it smelled of ammonia."

Because his family didn't have much money, Ludwigsen said, it wasn't a good thing when family members got sick.

"We had no medical insurance," Ludwigsen said. "When I was about 13 or 14, I told my mom my side hurt," he said. "She said to go to bed. Later, I complained again that it hurt bad. She told me to go to the hospital. There were no clinics in those days. We lived a mile from the hospital. When I got there, I stood at the counter and explained what the problem was. The doctor checked me out. He decided it was appendicitis. He operated on me. Then he called my Mom."

Another time, Ludwigsen said, he was "playing" with bullets.

"I would hit them with a hammer to hear them go off," he said. "One went into my knee. It felt funny and I had a hole in my pants. I had to go to the doctor for that too. He gave me a shot of Novocain. The skin swelled up and he cut out the bullet. He told me I would limp. But it didn't turn out that way."

Ludwigsen paid attention to the local aviation world as he grew up.

He remembered when the Pan Am flying boats – the Baby Clippers – came to Ketchikan in the late 1930s.

"They were Sikorskis, big damn things!" he said. "Ketchikan had a big, long float they could tie to. It was near Nordby's. You could watch the planes take off and land in the water. The planes were big monstrous silver things with round portholes! They had stewardesses that also had to be nurses. Everyone would watch the planes land and take off."

Later the Flying Boats docked in Ward Cove but then service was suspended during World War II. After the War, DC-4s were able to fly from Seattle to Ketchikan and Juneau and land at the airfields that were built during the War, so the flying boats never returned.

World War II

Like many Ketchikan residents who lived during the Great Depression, Ludwigsen divides his early life into the days before World War II and the days after.

Ludwigsen was 13 when America entered World War II.

"I can remember walking down the street when everybody said war was declared," he said. "That same night, the Deer Mountain cabin burned down. It was a great big, beautiful cabin on top of Deer Mountain. Some sucker went up there and burned it down and all the people in Ketchikan, including the Coast Guard, thought it was a signal for the Japanese to move in! It was serious business there for a while."

Ludwigsen said he immediately noticed that it became harder to move around the harbor because of wartime security. "The Navy set up this tower at Ryus Float," he said. "Any boat that wanted to move had to go to the tower and have someone stand on the dock and holler to the guy in the tower, where you were going, who you were and what your business was. Every boat had to do this in the harbor."

During the war, an airfield was built on Annette Island near Metlakatla, and a Canadian bomber squadron was located there. It was the only time in history that a foreign military base was established on United States soil.

"They would fly over Ketchikan and would practice air raids, dropping flour bags on us," he said. "Everybody in school would run like hell out of the way because we were being "bombed!" by the Japanese, supposedly. I've seen some crazy pilots in my day, but those Canadians were nuts! I mean those big twin-engine bombers at less than tree-top altitude, buzzing everything and dropping those goddamn flour sacks on everybody!"

Ludwigsen said the Navy requisitioned a couple of the airplane hangers in the harbor and based a pair of OX5 Kingfisher float planes there.

"One had a big pontoon under its body with two outrigger pontoons," he said. "Once when they were trying to load a 500-pound bomb it dropped into the water! I hope it was not armed and I assume they got it back."

He said that the military also hired several halibut schooners and turned them into patrol boats. Some had depth charges and others had machine guns. He said it was claimed that two of the converted schooners were responsible for sinking a Japanese submarine near Ketchikan.

Although the sunken submarine story is commonly repeated in stories about Ketchikan during the war, Historians have noted that a check of Japanese records after the war found no evidence of subs being lost in Southeast Alaska. Oddly, enough, a check of Russian records after the fall of the USSR found that a Russian submarine went missing off the Southeast coast during World War II.

Before, during and after the war, Ludwigsen was a commercial salmon troller. He remembered an incident involving one of the Canadian aircraft when they were based at Annette.

"I was fishing Stone Rock near Cape Chacon when a single engine Canadian Air Force fighter came streaking 100 feet above the water trailing black smoke!" he said. "It was going fast and heading straight home for the Annette Island field. It must have got close or made it. I never heard."

Because of his age, Ludwigsen had been too young to take part in the war, but many of the able-bodied men in the community who were of age were given deferments, at least initially, because the government wanted them to continue to commercial fish and supply salmon to feed the soldiers.

The salmon industry had been dropping from its peak in the early 1930s, primarily because of overfishing of the once seemingly limitless runs. But it picked up again in the early 1940s, when millions of cases of canned salmon were needed to supply the war effort.

Fishing and Fish Pirating in the 1940s

Ludwigsen fished with his Dad and his older brother Arnold, until he was 17.

"I fished with my brothers and my Dad every day when I was a little guy," he said. "Fished on their trollers, went out fishing all summer long. I didn't have time to play softball or baseball like other kids until I got to high school. I did a lot of rowing, going down the Cold Storage and back."

Ludwigsen's first boat had no name, only a registration number 31V37. It was 27-feet long.

It had an old gas engine in it. His father had gotten the boat from an older fisherman named Carl Jacobsen.

"It was tied up to my Dad's dock because he (Jacobsen) had nowhere to go, he had no money," Ludwigsen said. "So, my Mom and Dad took him in and helped him eat and played cards with him. When he died, he left the boat to my Dad, so that's the first one I fished with."

Ludwigsen said it was a challenging boat to get going.

"You had to put a pry in the flywheel to start it," he said. "It was a wet exhaust. Putt-putt-putt-putt. You had to pour a little gas in the snifter on the top of the cylinder, so she'd fire."

Ludwigsen said the 31V37 was a good boat.

"I did some good fishing, I almost sunk it once, full of Cohoes, at Cape Chacon, Stonerock," he said. "It was a little slow, my Dad used to tow me (with his boat). I remember leaving from Club Rocks near Duke Island in a heavy westerly and my Dad threw a line to me and I tied it to the bow, and he drug me clear across Clarence Strait to Stonerock Bay. And, you know, you can't leave the wheel when somebody's towing you. So, there I sat…for hours."

Ludwigsen said that what he most liked about the 31V37 was he could fish it by himself without needing any deckhands.

"I loved it because I could sit out on the back (deck) and let the fish bite if they want to," he said. "I was young enough to think 'oh this is wonderful.' But some of the time around Club Rocks, poor weather, and it was rolling. It was hard, trying to make a living. But I enjoyed it." Ludwigsen continued to fish during the summer.

Basketball

In the winter, he attended Ketchikan High School, where he was student body president and played forward on the Ketchikan High School basketball team, the Polar Bears.

"I started my freshman year, I was good enough to be on the second string," he said. "We traveled around to Petersburg, Metlakatla and Prince Rupert."

By his sophomore year, he was a starter.

"I won a lot of trophies and sportsmanship awards and all-star trophies," he said. "I really loved basketball!"

It was a more informal sporting world back then," Ludwigsen said. "Coaches and teachers would often use their own boats to take players to away games."

"The coach, old Mr. Hanna, we used to travel in his yacht," Ludwigsen said. "He'd pile all us kids on the damn boat, and we'd go to Petersburg, Wrangell, all the way to Juneau. Once we got stuck and had to anchor up in Taku Harbor and wait for the wind to calm down. We'd share cooking and chores. That was Victor Klose, Gus Olsen, Bob Crowder, Leif Leding and a whole bunch of us young guys. We had a good ball team. We won All-State twice."

After high school, Ludwigsen would continue to play for community basketball teams, including when he was living up in Bethel. His Ketchikan teams competed in, and won, the regional Lions Club Gold Medal Tournament in Juneau. After leading his team to numerous victories in the 1940s and 1950s, Ludwigsen was eventually named to the Gold Medal Hall of Fame. His teams also played against touring teams like the Harlem Globetrotters and the House of David.

"When you get to be as smart as I was them days, you are smarter than the teachers and you knew more than they did," he said. "One of my teachers, it was in civics class or something, I was fooling around in back not being my normal self. She stood me up in front of class and said, 'what did you come to school for?' and I said, 'to play basketball!' She said, 'Get out!' Out the door I went, and I never came back."

The Don Carlos

After high school, Ludwigsen got a larger power troller, the 36-foot Don Carlos.

"Asa Starkweather was an old-time fisherman, he had a boat called the Don Carlos that was tied along our float. When he decided to retire, I looked at the boat and it looked nice for me. Finally, Dad bought it for me."

Ludwigsen continued to fish until, as he puts it, the Army "rescued him" when he was drafted in December 1950. He said he had always figured he would be a fisherman for life, but he still occasionally had higher aspirations.

"I'd get to Chacon on my boat, the 'Don Carlos, I'd see airplanes flying by and I said, 'Boy that looks like an easy life up there!' " he said with a laugh.

In those days, Ludwigsen said, fisherman primarily fished in the summer, occasionally doing some fall king fishing, but never in the winter as is done now.

"Dad and Nels Nelson would fish over on Hadley (on Prince of Wales Island) in 90-fathom water, big kings there," he said. "Along that Grindle shore."

When asked about his favorite fishing spot in those years, Ludwigsen was cagey as most fishermen are.

"In the water," he said, before eventually conceding that the area around Cape Chacon on the southern tip of Prince of Wales Island was his favorite spot.

"Stonerock," he said. "Nichols Bay was tough because it was good (to fish) but too much of a westerly. Stonerock, because we could anchor in Stonerock Bay and there was a beautiful sandy beach and an old Indian village, a bunch of houses."

He noted that the weather on that part of Dixon Entrance was always dicey, particularly when a southeaster would brew up on the Canadian side of the border.

"You would have to beat it into Maclean's Arm or wherever," he said. "Whenever you'd see it coming. You could hear it coming via the radio, the Canadian fishermen down in Hecate Strait would broadcast: 'Yeah she's going about 25 to 30 knots here, but I got 34 kings on board."

When Ludwigsen would hear Canadian fishermen on the radio, there would be banter.

"Ed Alain and I, we'd tease them on the radio," Ludwigsen said. "Ed would say, 'Uh, hey Herman, I'm on the 'coffee grounds.' "You could hear those guys bragging down there."

By the mid to late 1940s, fish runs were rapidly decreasing in Southeast Alaska. The primary reason was the dozens of floating fish traps that had been placed along the salmon migration paths beginning in the early 1920s. Those traps provided a steady stream of salmon for the numerous canneries that operated in the Ketchikan area and helped boost the local economy leading some to call Ketchikan the "Salmon Capital of the World."

But the traps were also too efficient. Trap operators were supposed to allow enough salmon to escape past them and spawn future generations. But the pursuit of profit meant that the traps operated more than they should have. And when runs began decreasing in the late 1930s, the traps were kept open even longer, meaning that even fewer fish were reaching their streams.

That led many fishermen, particularly the salmon trollers, to do something that is now legendary in local history, become Fish Pirates.

It made perfect sense, if you couldn't find fish in the wild, you could certainly find them in the traps where they pooled until the cannery tenders could come along to scoop them out with nets or brail them as we called it and take them back to the canneries."

Fisherman learned that trap operators were not well paid and that a twenty-dollar bill, or more, could frequently convince a trap watchman to look the other way while someone brailed a few fish out of the trap.

If the trap watchman was not so pliable, fish pirates would sometimes nail a two-by-four to the watchman's cabin door to keep him locked in. Rarely, but occasionally, more violent steps would be taken.

Meanwhile, the canneries themselves would combat the more audacious pirates by hiring outside detectives to protect their fish. The locals called the outsiders "Pinkertons", whether they worked for the famous detective agency or not.

"Ed Alain and I were (pirates)," Ludwigsen said. "A lot of times we knew the Pinkerton's were after us. I would use one of Webber's airplanes and go out and scout around and land at a couple of traps and see if they wanted to sell any fish, but that didn't turn out too well there. We had one trap; it was a PAF (Pan American Fisheries) trap down by Moss Bay on Thorne Arm. He (the trap watchman) was getting to the point he didn't like twenty dollar or fifty-dollar bills. He needed hundred-dollar bills! He said he had too much money in the shack. He was selling to bigger boats too!"

Ludwigsen said the detectives were particularly interested in him because of rumors that he had cut the wire from a trap at Dall Head on Gravina Island.

Ludwigsen said that trap was actually vandalized by one of his former Kayhi classmates, but that the heat was on Ludwigsen anyway.

"We skedaddled out of there (Thorne Arm) and went north," he said. "We were anchored up in Tolstoi Bay (on Prince of Wales Island)," he said. "We were scared, we knew how the Pinkerton's worked; they were pretty sneaky. I didn't know what boats they had; you never knew. You didn't know where they were. Were they in the trap shack themselves? "

Like many of the fish pirates, Ludwigsen often knew the traps extremely well, having worked on the tenders that serviced them.

"Some of those traps I worked with FIP Cannery on the Sidonia, a tender, and we were brailing Onslow Island in that area up above Meyers Chuck," Ludwigsen said.

And for the most part, people in Ketchikan gave a "wink and a nod" to the activities of the fish pirates, because so many people were involved in the activity.

"A couple of times Ed Allain and I were laying in Pot Cove, near Lucky Cove, with our boats tied together, as it was too sloppy to go out and look," he said. "And in comes a cannery tender about 200 yards away from us. We were waving at them; they knew who we were. When you got a brailer hanging in the rigging, well things are (obvious)."

Ludwigsen said that Alain - who was an engine mechanic - was always trying to tune the Don Carlos' engine to get a little more speed. Ludwigsen said that meant maybe eight knots instead of the normal seven knots. And not always to beat the Pinkertons "Ed Alain and I tried to rebuild the engine in the Don Carlos for the Fourth of July Boat Races," he said. "We had some guy that was pretty hot, and he beat us by a little. Ed was tuning up everything and cleaning plugs because he knew my boat was fast."

After Ludwigsen returned from his military duty up North, he assumed he would return to fishing. But it was not to be.

"My Dad sold the (Don Carlos), he had to make the payment and I couldn't," Ludwigsen said. "He sold everything. It was all ready for fishing."

Always Looking to Fly

Ludwigsen was around 12 years old when he first caught the flying bug. He was attending White Cliff School in 1940 and had noticed planes flying nearby.

The Ludwigsen family lived on Tongass Avenue in those days and there was a small seaplane hangar down on the water side of the street.

"I would wander down there to hang around," he said. "A fella named Jimmy Reinhart asked me if I would like to go for an airplane ride. Being a young punk, crazy kid, I said sure and thought this was great! We got into a small yellow J2 Piper Cub with wooden floats and a wooden prop. It had a 45-horsepower Franklin engine with the pistons sticking out both sides of the cowling. We took off from the harbor and flew around town with me looking down at all the kids staring up at us. My eyes were as big as saucers. It was wonderful. I was sold on flying."

Ludwigsen immediately joined the group of local "ramp rats" who spent every free minute hanging out at the hangers, trying to be helpful. Pestering pilots like Herb Munter and Ray Renshaw for as many flights as possible.

"At the time, the US Army was on Annette island, they were building the airport," Ludwigsen said. "I got to fly back and forth to Annette in return for cleaning windshields and gassing planes. The airplanes being used were Skyrocket Bellancas, Pacemaker Bellancas, Vegas, Stinsons and just about anything that was known to fly."

Ludwigsen took his first flight lessons when he 16 with Jim Webber in 1944. Webber and Doc MacKenzie built a hanger near Ludwigsen's house at 1500 Tongass Avenue and started Webber Air Service.

"There again, with airplanes in my eyes, I was the first kid to be in the way, you might say," Ludwigsen said. "Helping Jim and Doc MacKenzie put the hangar up, like nailing shingles to the roof or whatever it took for them to let me hang around."

"Jim paid me $25 a week for helping out," Ludwigsen said. "This was great for me, getting paid to do what I wanted to do anyway. He took me for rides now and then and he would instruct me, teach me how to fly."

Ludwigsen's airtime was logged but he didn't "solo" with Webber. Then Pete Cessnun, a World War II bomber pilot, joined up with Jim Webber and Webber Air started a flight school.

"Pete was one of the major persons to give me all the flight training," Ludwigsen said. "The ups and downs of the airplane world. I soloed in four hours and some forty odd minutes. It was one of the fastest solos they'd ever had! They told me I was a natural. Another fella involved in my learning to fly the right way was Don Ross (A World War II fighter pilot).

I would say that I had the three best flight instructors in Southeast, or all of Alaska, Don, Pete and Jim."

Ludwigsen was still in high school at that point, where he was student body president, and a starting forward on the Ketchikan High School Polar Bears basketball team. He continued to fly, getting his private pilot's license and "ferrying" planes for Webber, mostly back and forth to Annette Island. Ludwigsen continued to spend time commercial trolling and flying whenever possible.

In 1948, Ludwigsen had his first inkling that flying could be dangerous.

A Pan Am DC-4 flying from Seattle to Annette got caught up in bad weather, trying to land and crashed into Tamgas Mountain near the airport on Annette. All 18 crew members and passengers were killed.

"I was in on the Pan Am crash on Tamgas Mountain," he said "We were in one of the first groups of the (Ketchikan) Rescue Squad. We were searching for that guy for a long time. The Coast Guard found him on top of the mountain. Dick Borch was running the rescue squad with Kenny Eichner. Borch and I and my brother Pete were the first guys to the site on the ground. That was a disaster, they were all gone. We went back later to retrieve the mail and all the other things we could find, including pieces of people. When you run into things like that you wonder 'is flying really worth it?'

Prior to finding the downed airliner, Ludwigsen spent time with Dick Berhoft on his boat, "Swift Sure", looking for the plane around Duke Island. It took several days to locate the plane after it went missing in the storm.

But the allure of flying was such a powerful draw, it was made clear in an October 1950 article in the Alaskan Sportsman magazine (the forerunner of Alaska magazine) written by Pete Cessnun, one of the pilots who trained Ludwigsen to fly and eventually – in the 1960s – hired him to work for Webber Air.

The article opens with a scene next to a campfire on Little Goat Lake in what is now Misty Fjords National Monument.

"Glancing across the red embers at my companion, Herman Ludwigsen, I could see his features highlighted by the flickering flames," Cessnun wrote. "The two of us here at this tiny lake, high in the mountains, surrounded by primeval wilderness as changeless and unchanged as it was centuries ago."

The two men were on a goat hunt, made possible by the float plane that had brought them there.

"Lashed to each pontoon was a nice, young, tender mountain goat," Cessnun wrote. "And in the co-pilot's seat, propped up as though ready to take over the controls, was a third. Next to a tiny lean-to which made our camp was still a fourth goat. Herman was to remain overnight at the site while I took advantage of the full moon to fly the other three goats to Ketchikan."

Cessnun went on to write rapturously about the previous week's deer hunt on Prince of Wales Island and a moose hunt.

"I never cease to be amazed by the variety of big-game animals and the sensational fishing made available by small planes from Ketchikan." Cessnun wrote. "In this country, where the only other means of transportation is by small boat, it seems miraculous to leave a first-class city with its modern conveniences and be landing within an hour on some lake full of fish near which big game abounds, unchanged by man."

Cessnun concludes his Alaska Sportsman article with a tale of taking Ludwigsen's troller, the "Don Carlos", on a moose hunting trip to Burroughs Bay (near the mouth of the Unuk River).

Saved by the Military and One Beautiful Girl

Then the military intervened. In 1950, he was drafted into the Army and sent to Fort Richardson in Anchorage for training. Ludwigsen says he was "saved" by the military from the life of being a fisherman. He spent the next two years as an Army "advisor" to a National Guard unit based in Bethel. Most of his time was spent as a mechanic for a crew that flew a Cessna 190 in the Yukon-Kuskokwim area that also worked to recruit area Natives to the National Guard.

"I flew a doctor and another guy into the villages in the Delta," Ludwigsen said. "Once native men said they would like to serve in the Army we would bring them in to the base. There a doctor gave them a physical which was easy to pass if you could walk and talk. If they could do that, they were officially in the 2nd Scout Battalion."

Flying in western Alaska was a lot different than what Ludwigsen was used to.

"It was a completely different kind of country in comparison to the Southeast," he said. "It was a real different way of life for me, from carrying honey buckets out of the house on a daily basis, to fighting off mosquitoes, who, by the way loved me. This was when I learned "white out" conditions in the Arctic for flyers, in wintertime. White out conditions means that the sky is gray, the ground is gray, there is no discernible horizon, making it impossible to know where the ground and sky meet."

It was in Bethel, in 1952, that Ludwigsen met his future wife Anita Joyce Lieb.

Herman and Ann have different memories of how they met.

"Shortly after I arrived in Bethel, I was walking down a mud road when I saw a young lady with gray parka and a wolf ruff coming towards me," Herman said. "Despite the fact that it was winter she wore light Capri pants and Capezo ballet slippers and no socks. I turned to my buddy, Amondo Scarfile and said to him "I'm going to marry that lady. "And Amondo Scarfile replied "You're out of luck as someone from the Signal Corps is chasing her.' "

Ann said she remembers things a little differently. Her dad owned the Tundra Shack, an ice cream parlor that also had a jukebox for dancing. She was 15 years old at the time and, as the oldest daughter, spent a lot of evenings running the Tundra Shack. She noticed Herman immediately when he came in.

"Oh my Gosh, he was handsome," she said. "He had on an Army uniform with a tight jacket. His buddy Scarfile introduced him to me, he thought I was 18. He started to visit me when I worked and soon, we were going for walks together while he showed me pictures of his family in Ketchikan. There was a certain self-confidence about him."

After four months, Herman asked Ann to marry him. He went to the Tundra Shack to ask her father. Her father told Herman to ask Ann's mother, who was out hanging up clothes. She said yes.

Ann was 15 and Herman was 24. Ann says that her parents were not concerned about the age difference.

"They really liked Herman, Mom and Dad," she said.

Although Ann's family, the Liebs, lived in Bethel when Herman arrived there in 1952, they were not from the area and they were not Yupik.

There were Inupiaq's from farther north.

"My grandfather (Samuel Anaruk) was an orphan," Ann said. "His family lived near Unalakleet and there was a big flu epidemic (in 1918-19) that killed everybody in his family except my grandpa. The church in Unalakleet took him in, raised him, taught him school, sent him to college and he became a school master. He married my grandma, and she became a schoolteacher and they taught from Little Diomede, all the little villages, all the way down to White Mountain."

Ann said she was born in White Mountain and then her family moved to the Bethel area.

"We had a walrus skinned boat," she said. "Even the dogs were in the boat. All of us, aunts, uncles, everyone. We came down the Fish River into Golovin Bay, into Norton Sound and followed the coast to St. Michaels, went up the Yukon, crossed over at Kalskag to the Kuskokwim River and eventually reached Bethel."

The family moved because her grandparents had teaching jobs outside of Bethel.

"We didn't stay in Bethel, we went to Nunapitchuk, right above Bethel, up the Johnson River," she said.

Her parents ended up teaching at a school in Kipnuk on the Bering Sea coast near Nunivak during World War II.

"My Mom and Dad, they taught school during the war because, I can only surmise, that (the authorities) didn't want to send white people up into the dangerous areas," she said. I was about four or five when we moved to Kipnuk and when we got back to Bethel, I was in the fourth grade."

Ann Ludwigsen said her father also had other jobs including doing administrative work for a regional airline.

After the war, her family settled in Bethel and her father bought "The Tundra Shack" in 1949 from the family of a teacher that was returning to Seattle.

"That's when we were introduced to hamburgers," Anita said. "It was different from Eskimo food. But I've lived this long because I ate real good Eskimo food for a lot of years!"

Ann's father expanded the Tundra Shack into a "roadhouse" that also provided lodging for travelers.

"Bethel was boozeless, but when I mention a roadhouse people would say '"oh, yeah, you grew up in a roadhouse,"' she said. "If they want to think that, let them."

After the Army, Back to Ketchikan

Herman Ludwigsen's tour of duty ended in 1952 and he signed up for four years with the Army reserve rather than re-up his regular

Army duty. His father-in-law bought Ludwigsen a Piper Super Cruiser on wheels.

As his Army time wound down, Ludwigsen had been planning to get an airplane and return to Ketchikan where he had learned to fly in the mid-1940s. He had his eye on a semi-derelict plane in Bethel.

"The plane was rough," he said. "The fabric was all ripped up; it had been sitting just off the dirt strip for years. It was a sad wreck. I could see it every time I went for a walk on the side of the runway and started asking questions.

The purchase price was $1,500, or $14,500 in 2020 dollars. And that was only the beginning, as Ludwigsen then spent four months rehabbing the Piper from the ground up.

"I rebuilt the whole thing," he said. "Rebuilt the engine, re-fabricated the fuselage. Your re-fabric jobs are tough, you have to stretch them tight, make sure all the joints, the connections, the tubing's are not rusted or corroded and fall apart on you. It was just a matter of doing the damn thing right."

When the plane was ready to fly, Ludwigsen was ready to head to Anchorage to get his Army discharge and then go home to Ketchikan, a distance of more than 1,100 miles, the longest flight distance he had flown up to that point.

"Flew the whole way without a radio," he said. "When you do that, you fly by the airport and let them know you need to make a landing, you make one pass on the downwind run and you blink your running lights and he sees you and he gives the red light, meaning 'don't land or go around'. Or gives you a green light, 'okay, come into land'. That was years ago, it happened that way because you don't have much communication."

Ludwigsen took off in inclement weather.

"My Dad said, '"You'll never see him again," Ann Ludwigsen said. "I said, 'oh yes, I will. "

Ludwigsen planned to fly first to McGrath, then Anchorage, then Yakutat, Juneau and finally Ketchikan.

"Anyone with any sense wouldn't have left," he said. "It was late November. I was on wheels, no skies, no radio, never having flown there before. (I was) just some dumb guy who took it and went. I can't believe it (now)!"

After flying past Aniak, Sleetmute, and Crooked Creek, he got into trouble.

"All hell broke loose," he said. "A big snow storm. (Later) looking at my charts, I wouldn't have made it anyway. I was flying ground contact. So, I turned back and landed at Crooked Creek. I overshot the runway because it was snowing heavily. Once I got on the ground I turned back."

He said the local schoolteacher in Crooked Creek came out to meet him.

"He looked at me and smiled," Ludwigsen said. "The Schoolteacher said 'Did you see that all the first 300 or 400 feet (of the landing) was all six-inch stumps? You're very lucky."

They had been extending the runway and had chopped down numerous alder trees but hadn't finished and the "runway" was filled with numerous stumps. Somehow, Ludwigsen's plane had dodged them all.

"It would have torn me apart!" Ludwigsen said.

The next day, he flew onto McGrath and then went through the Alaska Range via Ptarmigan Pass to Anchorage's Merrill Field.'

"It's kinda bumpy and rumpy flying through the Range and you hope to hell you get through to the other side," he said. "A lot of planes don't. There's a lot of pieces (of planes) there."

The weather from Anchorage to Yakutat was "sketchy" he said, but when he arrived in Yakutat, he was treated to a Thanksgiving dinner. There was heavy snow, again, between Yakutat and Juneau.

"The FAA in Juneau said 'Don't go' he said. "But I had to go; I want to go home. After I passed Cape Fanshaw, it was warmer."

The weather, he said, was generally good from there on to Annette Island.

Would he do that flight again, under those circumstances?

"Oh, hell no!" he said. "These days, I yell at guys for flying around here on wheels, just going to Petersburg or Wrangell!"

He was very happy to get to familiar territory.

"Annette was beautiful, two or three big runways," he said. "They (the Coast Guard at Annette) knew I was freshly discharged from the Army and they let me come in and hide out for the winter (leaving his plane in one of their hangers). In the Springtime, Captain comes and says 'Herman, you gotta go.' "

The Coast Guard needed the hanger, but Ludwigsen was already planning to get the plane to Ketchikan.

"I had never landed on a road before, but Larry Erickson and I went out to Mountain Point a few times to look and see where the wires were, which trees were leaning which way," he said.

He also had to convince the territorial highway patrol that it was okay to land on the dirt road on South Tongass Highway. Oral

Freeman - later Ketchikan mayor and state legislator - was the highway patrolman.

"I think he probably thought I was (crazy)," Ludwigsen said. "I said 'Oral, I gotta land here, it won't take long. Coming from up north, he maybe thought I did know something about landing in odd places on wheels."

Freeman and several of Ludwigsen's friends made sure the roadway was clear and he flew over.

"After I touched down, it seemed like everyday stuff," Ludwigsen said. "As far as I know, it's the only time a plane has landed on a Ketchikan highway!"

But it wasn't everyday stuff to both Ketchikan newspapers, the Chronicle, and the Daily News, printed stories on the landing.

The Daily News, which had been advocating for an airport on Revillagigedo Island proudly noted the first landing on the "Mountain Point airport!"

The Chronicle also considered it a milestone.

"When Herman Ludwigsen landed his 3-place Piper Cruiser plane at Mountain Point yesterday, he was not instituting a new mail-passenger service to the burgeoning community," the Chronicle noted. "Instead, he had been forced to move the wheeled plane from its hanger on Annette."

In those days, Mountain Point - five miles south of Ketchikan - considered itself a suburb of Ketchikan with a small grocery store, a church, a roadhouse, and a residential area.

After landing, Ludwigsen removed the wings from the Piper and brought them into Ketchikan and stored them at the family boathouse. Later he re-installed the wings, causing him to go back through the tedious process of putting the fabric on the wings, with the help of local seamstress Harriet Olson.

"Had to rebuild the wings, that took a long time," he said. "Had to buy fabric to re-cover the wings and sew the fabric on with big, long needles. I would push the needle through and Harriet on the other end would grab it, make sure the rip stitching was over the ribs. Real tough stuff. You had to make sure the fabric doesn't rub on the wing strut or the rib. You have to make it tight."

Within a few months, Ludwigsen had also purchased and installed floats on the Piper.

Ludwigsen eventually sold the Piper, and it was taken to Anchorage, where it was destroyed in a crash.

"I got a message, someone sent me a little ID tag (from the inside of the cockpit door)," Ludwigsen said. "It said 'Herman, here is what is left of your plane."

But he noted that the serial number was transferred to a new plane.

It would be another 20 years before the current Ketchikan International Airport was built on Gravina Island, a short ferry ride from Ketchikan's West End, ending the need for future pilots to land on local roadways or beaches to reach Ketchikan.

The early 1950s were a busy time in Ketchikan's growing floatplane industry. In fact, the locals began referring to the planes as "air taxis" because they were often used to shuttle people and supplies to the far-flung logging camps and fishing canneries in the region. More flights also meant more plane crashes and almost immediately Ludwigsen developed a reputation as someone who could find down planes and aviators.

His first "recovery" was that of pilot Don Bilderback and his girlfriend in their Cessna 140. The plane had crashed on Karta Lake on Prince of Wales Island.

"Don and his brother Ed owned a fishing boat and used the plane for fish spotting," Ludwigsen said. "Ed came to see me one morning and told me that Don had gone on a trout fishing trip to Karta and hadn't returned yet."

Ludwigsen and Ed Bilderback flew over to Karta Lake.

"I learned something on this trip, don't ever have a relative with you," Ludwigsen said. "I don't want a brother with me ever again, who gets to see his brother still strapped in his seat, under 10 feet of water, in a wrecked plane. It isn't a nice sight. The girl was also there. Still strapped in."

Ludwigsen believes they hit a tree while landing on the lake and spun straight down into the water.

A second crash, a short time later had a better outcome. Ludwigsen can't remember the name of the pilot & his son, who were involved, but remembers that they were part of a flying club on Annette Island that owned a Piper J3 Cub. The crash had happened on Downdraft Lake on Gravina Island.

"He (the pilot) had made an approach to the lake and screwed it up," Ludwigsen said. "He crashed on landing; they didn't get hurt. I found the plane in the lake but didn't land because I didn't see anyone. I flew the beaches down to Bostwick Inlet, figuring that, if they were able, it would be reasonable for them to walk out, which they did."

He found the pilot and his son by a fire on the beach.

"He says 'Herman, you can have the airplane, I don't want no part of it!" Ludwigsen said. "So, I thought I'd become the owner of a second airplane. Lo and behold the rest of the club members said 'No, it's our plane, you can't have it."

Ludwigsen did fly an inspector from the Civilian Aeronautics Board (CAB) to the lake to see the plane and the inspector concluded the crash was "pilot error."

"Just a new flyer trying to do something he shouldn't have," Ludwigsen said. "Which is usually the case in most airplane crashes."

Over his flying career, Ludwigsen became well known for finding downed planes and people lost in the wilderness. He said it's because he always "liked to fly low."

"I don't like to fall too far!" he said with a laugh. "I just feel better flying at tree level. I don't want to fly at 10,000 feet, I like to fly ground contact so I can see things. That's why I have been so lucky in finding people." Ludwigsen said that flying "low" in general and keeping your eyes open was always good for safer flying.

"You always wanted to look for a landing spot if you needed it in an emergency," he said. "You were always eyeing places and thinking 'I could land there if I had to."

The third crash was much more serious and more famous. It involved the President of Condor Petroleum Ellis Hall who crashed his twin engine plane near Boca de Quadra in August of 1953.

Finding the wreckage of Hall's plane put some attention on Ludwigsen's burgeoning career, but not all the attention was good.

Since the Hall crash focused some attention on Ludwigsen, he decided it was a good time to get his commercial pilot's license. He had been unofficially guiding hunters and fishermen for a couple of years.

"I was cheating the government," he said. "That's normal for everybody anyhow. I didn't have a commercial license, but I had an airplane and knew a lot about hunting and fishing. I was taking guys out hunting and fish-spotting for fishermen like Dick Sanchez and Nels Nelson and all the boys. Making some money that way."

But then he was reminded of the tenuousness of his position.

"I believe I had accumulated around 2,000 hours by then," Ludwigsen said. "One day, Hap O'Brien of the CAA (Civil Aeronautic Authority) came down from Anchorage, tapped me on the shoulder and said 'Herman, I think you'd better get a commercial license,' of which I took immediate heed."

Ludwigsen went south to Hank Riverman's Lake Union Air Service and got his commercial float plane license. But the local air taxi world was crowded with new pilots in the post war years.

"I couldn't make enough to live on " Ludwigsen said.

So, in the spring of 1956, he went south again, this time to Boeing Field in Seattle. He got his instrument rating and his multi-engine sea and land ratings, making him qualified to operate just about any plane in Alaska.

"I came home with a pair of wings on my forehead thinking I'd never have trouble getting a job." Ludwigsen said.

The job he really wanted was to fly the twin-engine Grumman Goose used by the rapidly expanding Ellis Airlines, which was becoming the dominant air service in the region.

Ellis had been formed in the early 1930s, not long after Naval Aviator Bob Ellis had arrived in Ketchikan. By the 1950s, Ellis had purchased several military surplus Goose and - along with Alaska Coastal in Juneau - was dominating air travel in Southeast and northern British Columbia. Ludwigsen wanted to fly for Ellis. But Ellis and his chief pilot Bud Bodding had other ideas.

"They figured I was still a wild-eyed young kid and didn't think I was here to stay, as a pilot, and wouldn't hire me," Ludwigsen said.

Bethel Charter Service

With his new ratings, there was no point in Ludwigsen staying in Ketchikan and flying single engine floatplanes. He went north and - with a letter of recommendation from Ellis - secured a job with Wein Alaska Airlines in Fairbanks.

"I was under the impression I would be flying Norsemans and Gull Wing Stinsons from Fairbanks to Circle City, Central and Eagle, all over the upper Yukon on bush runs," Ludwigsen said. But Wien had other ideas.

"After reviewing my additional licenses, they stuck me on a C46 (a large military twin engine transport plane) flying the Distant Early Warning Line which was being built at the time. I became disinterested in a hurry, flying 14,000 pounds of steel and stuff to these out of the way places, or sites, between Barter Island, Barrow, Wainwright, on instruments, in snow, and buzzing airports chasing caribou and reindeer off of them so we could land the contraptions."

Ludwigsen said he never really enjoyed flying the large planes. As a result, unlike many other local pilots, he never really hankered to moving on up to jets when Alaska Airlines came in and purchased Alaska Coastal Ellis (the companies had merged in the early 1960s) and replaced with Goose flights with jet service. Flying in northern Alaska also meant flying in white out conditions, in which the gray of the sky merged with the gray of the land.

"Personally, my love of flying includes being able to see the ground when I fly," Ludwigsen said.

Flying on "instruments" was also frequently necessary on the northern coasts, as was using "dead reckoning" sometimes.

"There was no heat in the planes over the clouds at 10,000 to 12,000 feet," Ludwigsen said. "One of the needles on the indicator pointed to the ass end of what we passed, and the next arrow pointed to where we were going. There were times when we had a big ass load of steel so that the arrow needles froze and did not move. Captain George Clayton would time us and when he was sure we passed Barrow, according to wind and drift. Then we would be out over the Arctic Ocean and we would fly for a half an hour or so we knew there were no mountains we could hit. He would drop the plane down over the ice and soon the needles would thaw out and we could find Barrow."

Ludwigsen said he had always wanted to fly with Wien because of an advertisement he had seen when he was a child.

"It had Eskimo drums beating and I wanted to be a part of it," he said. But when it was clear he wouldn't be flying bush planes, he left, He said it was also hard to stay there in Fairbanks because there was no public transportation between the town and the airport, and he couldn't find good housing.

In leaving Wien, Ludwigsen knew he couldn't go back to Ketchikan and make a living flying. So, he returned to his wife's home in Bethel, where he and his father- in-law, Max Lieb, started up Bethel Charter Service.

"Max provided the financial backing and I flew the plane," Ludwigsen said. "It was a very prosperous business until I moved our family back to Ketchikan in 1965." In Bethel, Ludwigsen's Cessna 180 was parked in front of the family house on the Kuskokwim River year-round. It was on floats in the summer months and on skis in the winter.

"It was an education for me, being a bush pilot in western and northern Alaska, flying in snow and white out conditions, always an immediate danger," Ludwigsen said. "It was below zero freezing cold in the winter and putting up with the ever-present mosquitoes in the summer months. It was a continual job in the winter just keeping the plane in flying condition; getting up way before daylight to firepot the engine so it would start; draining the oil at night so it wouldn't turn to hard bacon grease. We didn't have a hangar. No one did in those days."

Ludwigsen's second stint in Bethel began in 1956. It also coincided with the beginning of family life. Bethel Charter Service was a family affair for Herman, Ann and their three children. Their home on the river was the base for the airline with Ann doing the bookkeeping and handling the radios. She was also the "gas boy" and the freight delivery person. It was her job to take care of everything besides the mechanics and the flying, giving Herman plenty of time to fit in as many "revenue" flights each day would allow.

Bethel Charter Service operated for seven years, year-round. "I was young and like all young folks, thought I was indestructible and could take the strain and pressure of flying those long hours with impunity to my physical self," Ludwigsen said. "I flew in the summer months an average of 8 to 10 hours a day. It was great. Life was wonderful for Ann and me. We made a lot of money and kept putting it back into the business."

It also helped that Ann's family was well known throughout the area.

"My father-in-law was a storekeeper, hotel keeper, fur trader, restaurant owner and besides all this, he had the only place in town where young kids could go to dance to a jukebox, eat hamburgers and ice cream," Ludwigsen said. "Max made his own ice cream. Consequently, I became known throughout the Yukon/Kuskokwim Delta, to the Yupik population, as 'The Akutag-Suun Nengauk.' In other words, the 'Ice Cream Maker's Son-in-Law.'"

Flying in Bethel meant that Ludwigsen had to learn to fly in a different environment than in Southeast. For one thing, there was the whiteout conditions, but there was also the challenge of the extremely low temperatures, minus 20 and 30 degrees, much lower than the milder Southeast winters. There was also the challenge that sometimes supplies, like oil, were not up to par.

"I was at Kipnuk, a village on the coast, to pick up people when I need to refuel as I had flown more than I anticipated," Ludwigsen said. "I asked the guy (at the school) if I could buy some fuel from him and he said sure. The 50-gallon barrel with the hand pump was over by the generator. I smelled the fuel; it was 25-30 degrees below zero and it only smelled like an oil-based product. I noticed his generator was belching black smoke and coughing, but I thought nothing of it."

So, he filled the wing tank.

"Soon, fat, dumb and happy I was airborne with three passengers on board," he said. "Two of them were going to get married in Bethel, 90 miles away." Halfway to Bethel he switched to the tank with the Kipnuk fuel.

"The plane started to lose power, gulp and backfire and I could not keep it in the air," Ludwigsen said. "Down we came. It was flat country, and we came down on a little lake. I kept the engine running and tried to taxi to the small village of Tuntuliak, but our engine quit."

The wind was blowing, so Ludwigsen built an ice bridge to secure the plane.

"I cut down into the ice about a foot and then went over a foot and cut down again," he said. "Next I had to try to go across so I could put a rope under the ice bridge. I had to make sure at least one of the holes reached the water so when I got the rope through the ice bridge, I poured water over my planes skis and then filled the holes I cut for the bridge."

Then they sat and waited because their radios were not working well enough to call out.

"We sat all afternoon and night and half the next day," he said. "I was lucky that I had my new mukluks (he had purchased in Kipnuk) and the fur parka my mother-in-law had made for me."

He said his Eskimo passengers were also well dressed and unconcerned about the weather or the wait.

"They were quiet and tranquil," Ludwigsen said. "The inside of the plane was frosted up from us breathing. We ate frozen beans and candy bars."

He said that his family back in Bethel was concerned when he didn't return and initiated a search that eventually found the downed plane.

"I was never so glad to have a 180 flying along looking for us " he said. "We had to make two trips to get all of us back to Bethel, but it was a good thing we did because a big snowstorm came that night and nothing moved for a few days."

Later, Ludwigsen determined that the problem was the gas that was in the 50-gallon drum was kerosene, not gasoline.

"It was not hot enough to spark," Ludwigsen said. "I learned the hard way to be careful of the fuel I put in the airplane as everyone does not know what type they have."

Ann had been in the search plane, even though she was pregnant with her third child.

Which naturally raises the question. Was she ever nervous about Herman flying and what could happen?

"No," she said recently. "I knew he was a really good pilot."

Besides, she noted, she was raised around planes and took her first flight to Kipnuk when she was four years old. Flying was just a natural part of life when she was growing up.

Operating a flight service in western Alaska in those days often meant that sometimes you didn't do things exactly by the book.

"I got a couple of contracts to the villages and get National Guard troops which was fine, but they had too much stuff" Ludwigsen said. "Since the river was frozen, I had Albert Schmitt, the water hauler, take his flat-bed truck on the frozen river and transport the luggage. I just transported the people. Soon the National Guard in Anchorage found out and they were unhappy. Your contract says you must transport people and luggage."

Ludwigsen pointed out that the contracts did not say the people and luggage had to be transported by air.

"The next year the contracts said 'fly people and baggage' " he said. "I did not get any more contracts because they were mad at me."

It was one of a couple of times, he said, where the rules were changed because of something he did.

Another time, he tried to do a good deed and it cost him.

"A couple of young trappers came to Max and me in Bethel with traps and food enough to live out (in the wilderness) for a month." he said. "They did not have a dog sled. They wanted me to come back in a month; they were there when I arrived. We had to take out the back seat of the airplane so they could get all their gear in, that meant that one guy had to sit on the gear without a seat belt."

When they arrived back in Bethel, they were met by a man with the Civil Aeronautic Administration (the forerunner of the Federal

Aviation Administration). He was fined $900 for not having the second seat belt.

"There was a big storm coming." Ludwigsen said. "If I had of left the one guy, he would have died."

And there were times that Ludwigsen, the old fish pirate, helped people evade the authorities.

"One spring in Bethel there was a lot of bootlegging going on." he said. "The FBI and State Troopers were watching the planes that came from Anchorage."

Bootleggers would charter into Anchorage and load up with booze and then return to Bethel making a lot of money."

Ludwigsen said that Chet Alkins chartered him and was bringing nine cases of alcohol back, but clearly was aware that something was up. He asked Ludwigsen to take him, instead, to Oscarville, a village 20 miles from Bethel.

"He unloaded his booze," Ludwigsen said. "Then we flew to Bethel."

It was springtime, and there was "overflow" on the still frozen river.

"It is hard enough to land in the center, but the tide comes in and puts two or three feet of water between the ice where the plane is and the bank" Ludwigsen said.

"In fact, the edges were soft. Usually, two or three inches of snow would freeze on top of this overflow, but it was not enough to hold a man's weight."

Because the authorities were expecting Alkins to be bringing booze in, there was someone waiting when they arrived.

"Ann watched out the window as the FBI guy came down to arrest Chet and me." Ludwigsen said. "He fell through the ice. Soon he was able to crawl back to the solid snow on the shore. He glanced once and saw there was no booze on the plane and left town muttering something."

During the late 1950's and early 1960's, oil exploration was picking up in Alaska and some of Ludwigsen's early clients were Amerada Hess and Shell Oil. Both companies were curious about potential oil deposits in the Kuskokwim drainage.

They didn't find much oil but did come across significant coal deposits. Over time Ludwigsen became friends with oilmen like head geologist Ralph Rudeen and Bob Payne of Shell Oil.

From 1959 to 1961, Ludwigsen had a contract with Payne to fly exclusively for Shell Oil. He received $5,000 a month plus expenses to fly.

"By this time, we had been able to lease a second (Cessna) 180." Ludwigsen said. "Ann and I hired a pilot to take care of business in the Bethel area, while I was off with the geologists, looking for oil from Kotzebue to Fort Yukon and on up to Prudhoe Bay. Ann, by this time, had her own regular job with Northern Consolidated Airlines (in Bethel) as the radio/teletype operator."

Back in Bethel, Bethel Charter Service's main competition was Samuelson Flying Service, owned by Bethel native, Jimmix Samuelson.

"It must be said, Jimmix was a homegrown pilot from one of the old families in Bethel and he actively and loudly resented my presence in Bethel as 'gussuck' (white person) competition." Ludwigsen said. "He spoke Yupik fluently and naturally I didn't. There were a lot of times, with me standing right in front of him, when he would try to talk an Eskimo out of flying with me. All this in Yupik, and my passengers would tell me what he said, in flight. A lot of people were bilingual in the Bethel area, and a whole lot spoke only Yupik, but they respected Max and since I was married to his daughter, I was accepted."

In flying for Standard Oil as well, Herman helped with Neil Smith's "gravity meter" survey of the Yukon, Bristol Bay and Kuskokwim areas.

"We had to land every mile on floats," Ludwigsen said. "Neil would get on tundra, set up his instruments. He did this every mile to Bristol Bay. Then we flew back from Bristol Bay to Port Heiden on the Chain (Aleutian Islands). We landed in a lake close to the (Port Heiden) school. We had a lot of red tape on the plane. The schoolteacher thought I was a Russian; he came out of the school with a gun."

Being gone so often made it hard to connect with family at times, Ludwigsen said, adding that after one extended period of work for the oil companies, he came home only to discover that his youngest child, Jocelyn, didn't recognize him.

In Bethel, the Ludwigsen's had one of the nicest homes and a steady stream of visiting friends, many in the aviation world.

"Wonderful people like Jimmy and Dorothy Hoffman, Alice (Jimmix's sister) and Ray Miller and Howard and Sally Elliot," Ludwigsen said. One reason that the Ludwigsen house was so popular was that Herman had installed a 500-gallon water storage tank and put in something that few local houses had in the late 1950s, running water.

"This enabled us to buy one of those metal, stand-up showers from Sears Roebuck so we could take regular showers," Ludwigsen said. He also installed a flush toilet, in order to get rid of a common Bethel appliance, the "Honeybucket".

Unfortunately, having water delivered proved expensive and they went back to the Honeybucket.

"Since we had the only shower in town, whenever our friends stopped in for a drink or coffee, our shower became very popular." Ludwigsen said. "We had very clean friends. Their kids and ours were in the same general age group so there were a lot of dinners between the families."

Around this time, Ludwigsen continued his knack for finding downed aircraft. His work locating a downed Air Force C123 Cargo master even made the local papers back in Ketchikan, as well as the Seattle Post-Intelligencer.

"A few weeks ago, Ludwigsen rated headlines in Anchorage for his rescue of 11 persons aboard a C123 which crashed on a frozen riverbed near Bethel," the Ketchikan Daily News noted in April of 1960. "Ludwigsen heard the (mayday) call and was beside the C123 within 20 minutes. Personnel of the Air Force base in Bethel honored the rescue pilot at a dinner. In a letter to his parents (in Ketchikan) Ludwigsen indicates that making a speech at the dinner was a tougher assignment than the rescue flight had been!"

Ludwigsen said that the C123 was hit by a gust of wind on takeoff from Cape Romazof, a Cold War radar site, and bounced off the runway and back into the air causing the right landing gear to collapse and fuel tank to rupture. The plane was able to stay in the air for 20 minutes while the pilot looked for a safe place to land. Eventually he had to put the plane down blind.

"He had no choice in the matter, but to let it down through blowing snow with 1/2-mile visibility." Ludwigsen said. "He didn't know what was ahead of him. Luckily, he barely cleared the 'mud volcanoes' (a series of three small mountains in the area) and landed on the only possible straight stretch around, which was a frozen slough bed. He made a gear up landing and slid to a stop before coming to the edge of the slough bank."

Ludwigsen was in the area with his 180 and the CAB told him to look for the downed C123. He landed near the larger plane - he said it was easy to spot because of its orange tail. He then assisted the captain and used his radio to safely guide two Northern Consolidated rescue planes to the area. The crew was flown back to Bethel.

The C123 stayed on the ice for a month. The Air Force returned to the downed aircraft to check the ice thickness and to mark a landing strip. The Air Force built a repair station for the plane despite the temperatures in the 20-25 below zero range. The C123 was eventually put back together and flown to Anchorage.

Around that time, Bob Hope chose the King Salmon Air Force base for his annual serviceman's show, Ludwigsen said. Bethel Charter flew two local servicemen to King Salmon for the show. Ann went too. Ludwigsen said that besides Hope, the show included Jerry Colona, Frances Langford, and Martha Rae, among others. "As we walked in, I was wearing a fur parka that my mother-in-law had made for me which had a large wolf ruff," Ludwigsen said. "And Bob Hope made a comment, something to the effect of referring to me as an arriving wolf, and he duly thanked us for bringing the two airmen from Bethel. It was really nice."

Meanwhile, Ludwigsen continued adding to his seemingly endless tales of rescues and recoveries. In the Spring of 1957, he found longtime Alaskan bush pilot Bob "Bald Eagle" Curtis. Curtis was flying a twin-engine Widgeon for Ramstad Construction out of Anchorage on a passenger/cargo flight from Anchorage to Bethel to Nunivak Island where Ramstad was building an airport at Mekoryuk. Besides passengers, the flight involved frozen meat including turkeys, ham, and wieners.

"Curtis was a good friend of Max's so when he failed to arrive on Nunavik as scheduled - this was about 18 hours later - they called Max." Ludwigsen said. "Max sent me along with my friend and helper Jackie Stewart to search for Bob. After two hours of searching in the Baird Inlet area, we found him. He was okay. The first thing the 'Bald Eagle' said was 'Sure glad to see you, I'm tired of eating frozen wieners!' "

Ludwigsen said that Curtis had lost one of the engines in flight and had to land.

Then, In the summer of 1962, Ludwigsen and Lieb lost Bethel Charter Service after a bad crash that killed a company pilot and two Department of Fish and Game employees.

"I had been flying very long hours for quite a while and was getting pretty tired and not feeling well." Ludwigsen said. "So, I went to see a doctor, the only one in Bethel who treated Caucasians. She examined me and decided to give me an (electrocardiogram) at which time she told me that I had had a mild heart attack, Naturally, both my wife and I were stunned."

Ludwigsen then hired a fill in pilot, Tommy Conquest, while the Ludwigsen's decided what to do.

"I just couldn't imagine life without being an aviator. Ludwigsen said. "It was my whole working life."

Unfortunately, Conquest and two Fish and Game employees died when the Bethel Charter Service plane crashed on a fish watching trip on a stream near Quinhagak.

"Since I was home most of the time, I listened mainly to our aircraft radio, so when the preacher from Quinhagak called I was the one to hear the bad news firsthand after the crash." Ludwigsen said. "(the preacher) told me my airplane had gone by the village and then some black smoke was reported from the direction it had gone. I chartered a plane and flew right down. Sure enough, Tommy had flown right into the ground."

Ludwigsen said that he believes that Conquest was distracted by the fish counting activities and stalled the plane. All three men were killed instantly.

"Bethel Charter was just about $5,000 short of being free and clear of any debts when this happened," Ludwigsen said.

A dispute arose over the company's insurance and it was determined by the insurance company that the liability did not apply to any pilots other than Ludwigsen. Both the state and the families of the Fish and Game workers sued Bethel Charter.

"We lost everything and had to start over," Ludwigsen said.

In the meantime, Ludwigsen discovered, when he went to another doctor in Anchorage, that the heart attack diagnosis was incorrect.

"I went to Anchorage and had my doctor give me a good going over and he said there was nothing wrong with me. " Ludwigsen said. "I was required to go to three different physicians before my airman's medical certificate was reinstated. They all concurred that in fact I had not suffered a heart attack. I had been suffering from extreme fatigue."

One of Ludwigsen's good friends, the chief pilot for Northern Consolidated, Jimmy Hoffman, helped Ludwigsen get back in the game by hiring him to fly mail runs up and down the Kuskokwim and Yukon rivers.

"He checked me out in the Bamboo Bombers, which are UC-78, twin engine old type aircraft used in World War II by the Army and Navy as trainers." Ludwigsen said. "They had 300 (horsepower) Lycoming engines with Hartzell props. It was a fantastic old piece of machinery. It was very interesting. These planes were already an antique by that time."

Shortly after Ludwigsen began flying for Northern Consolidated, he was on a return flight to Bethel from Hooper Bay and Chevak.

"The weather was real crummy" he said. "Low ceilings and squally icing conditions."

He was flying a twin-engine plane, which he said was better equipped for the condition. While enroute a plane following him piloted by Gary Hodges called him to ask about the weather. Ludwigsen suggested he head to the north to Devil's Elbow on the Yukon River and take the longer route to the Kuskokwim where the weather seemed to be better.

Instead, Hodges continued to fly behind Ludwigsen on the more direct route to Bethel. After Ludwigsen arrived in Bethel, the local FAA officials asked him to go back out and search for Hodges' plane which had been out of contact for nearly an hour.

"He had hit the frozen tundra straight down." Ludwigsen said. "Apparently he lost visibility in white-out conditions. The aircraft was scattered over a wide area with no survivors. Three people were killed."

In the Spring of 1963, Ludwigsen found an overdue miner and his "Cat train" on the Kuskokwim River. Albert Kvamme was coming down from the Kilbuck Mountains to Akiak.

"He was on a D8 Caterpillar tractor pulling his house and supplies on a sled, in other words, a Cat train." Ludwigsen said, and had gotten delayed because of overflow water on the edges of the frozen river. Ludwigsen flew out in a Northern Pilatus Porter and found that Kvamme was okay. "These are the kind of searches any of us pilots liked the best."

Time to Head Home

Ludwigsen said he enjoyed working with the people in the Yukon-Kuskokwim area but found the region a "primitive, Godforsaken place." By 1965, the family had decided their children needed better schooling. It was time for the Ludwigsen's to return to Ketchikan.

"Ann came to Ketchikan with the kids for school." Ludwigsen said. "A few months later I came down. Carl Mazoni, one of my best friends, died in a plane crash on Deer Mountain. He was flying for Webber. I was asked to come back to fill his spot. I took the job."

Pete Cessnun was running Webber Air at the time. Webber was the main aviation contractor at the Pulp Mill. Don Ross was the chief pilot and checked Ludwigsen out. The first trip was on a Cessna 172, first passenger was Margaret Bell, the doyenne of Loring and Ketchikan's most famous author. Pete had been her favorite pilot but thereafter Herman flew her to Loring.

"From then on, I was her chief pilot." Ludwigsen said. "Whenever Maggie wanted to fly to or from Loring, it was always Webber Air and please send Herman." In the early days, Ludwigsen usually flew five days a week.

"The pay wasn't much," he said. "It was a job. In them days, things were hard enough, so we kept on going."

Ludwigsen said the pay was a flat $700 a month, about $5,000 in 2020 dollars, but the hours were long, frequently 12-15 hours a day when the weather and daylight allowed.

Webber continued to expand to service the logging camps in the area, Ludwigsen said, acquiring two larger Cessna 185s.

"It was a very busy company with the pulp mill getting rolling then," Ludwigsen said. "It kept airplanes in the air continuously back and forth. Fighting the weather and whatever."

After a few years, Don Ross sold his stake in Webber Air to Cessnun, and Ludwigsen became Webber's chief pilot.

"Pete was negotiating to buy a Grumman (Goose) to carry bigger loads back and forth to camps, when you couldn't get things up into a Beaver or 185," Ludwigsen said. "He had contacted a guy up at Boeing Field who was rebuilding a Grumman from the ground up. Sent me down there to look. You could walk between the ribs and the belly, had it all apart. Pete wanted it after I said it looked good."

It proved to be Ludwigsen's favorite Goose, likely his favorite plane, 045, which crashed later with a different pilot.

"She was a fine bird," Ludwigsen said.

When Ludwigsen took his first flight in the Goose, three Ellis pilots came over and went for the test ride.

"Had a little accident with it," Ludwigsen said. "The Grumman are noted for leakage in the hull. They have about nine small holes in the bottom in each section of the belly that you can unscrew a nut and drain the water out. And then make sure you put that bolt back in the hole otherwise you might do a little fishing with the airplane. But Pete being nervous started everything going and forgot the bolts. When I applied the power to the plane everything went to the tail end, all the water and there was quite a bit of water in the airplane and the Ellis pilots were jumping around trying to keep out of the water and I taxied it to the pullout and let it drain out and flushed it out with freshwater.

"You have to remember to pre-flight your airplane," Ludwigsen added. "Don't forget. Things happen when you don't."
Although Ludwigsen loved flying the Grumman Goose, comparing its powerful engines to a freight train, like all planes it had its quirks. For example, a single alternator for the two engines. Which meant it was sometimes hard starting particularly in cold weather.

So sometimes, a Goose pilot would have to resort to that most basic actions of early flight, hand cranking the props.

"I was called to go to Tuxekan where Hagen and Sundstad had a logging camp and they had injuries," Ludwigsen said, adding that because the Goose had folding seats it was uniquely equipped to handle stretchers. "When I landed there everything was fine. I got to the dock and they came down with the two guys on stretchers and the nurse and put them in the airplane for me, laid them down behind me."

But when he went to take off, the engines refused to start.

"I slid over the the right side - the co-pilot's side - opened the window and reached up and grabbed the prop," Ludwigsen said. "The Pratt and Whitney 985, 450 horses don't have any compression until it has started and then when she goes, you stay away from it. Anyway, I reached out and grabbed the prop blade and give it one hard flip up and she started just like that, because it was warm."

Then he switched over to the pilot's seat and did the same thing. "I flipped it up and it fired," he said. "Mechanics had to change the alternator when we got to town. As far as dead engines, it's normal, you just take care of it."

But he conceded that hand cranking a Goose prop was not as easy as all that.

"You better learn, stay clear of the damn thing when spinning that prop," he said. "Sometimes they'll backfire and drag you right with it. Just enough (of the arm has to be out the window) to get the tip of the blade. More than that and you'll be in trouble."
The Goose quickly became the workhorse of the Webber fleet. So much so, that the airline eventually added a second one. The booming timber industry had become the economic engine that drove the Southeast Alaska economy and Webber Air rode that economic wave.

"This was a time when logging was done from float camps, with A-frame's logging off salt water," Ludwigsen said. "The airplane pilot, upon arriving at any camp, dropped the mail off and hit the cookshack and was treated royally, just like a king. We had coffee and were eating cakes, cookies, pies. And if we hit a camp on Saturday just before shutdown for the weekend, it was steak dinner for sure. Everyone worked hard in the logging camps and they lived good. They earned it."

Meanwhile, Ludwigsen continued to rescue people who had come to grief.

"One day, I took off with a fully loaded Beaver headed for Thorne Bay and by Channel Island, right outside of Ward Cove, looked down and saw some gas cans floating in the water and a boat upside down," Ludwigsen said. "It was windy, blowing like hell, so I thought I'd better land and see what it was and sure enough here is some old fella named Sutherland hanging onto a gas can and had been in the water for about 30 minutes. He was really cold and stiff, the old bugger."

Ludwigsen flew the old man back to town and gave him some of his clothes and warmed him up the airline's furnace room.

"(We) offered to take him to the hospital to make sure he was okay, but he declined saying 'heck no, I'm tough enough,' " Ludwigsen said. "A few weeks later, he sent my clothes back with his thanks."

Another incident involved fellow Webber pilot Mark Easterly, who crashed in the trees near Big Salt on this way to Port Alice to pick up some loggers.

"He didn't damage the plane too much and he didn't hurt himself," Ludwigsen said. "Steve Cagley (later a jet pilot for Alaska Airlines) was my ramp rat. He was my spotter. We saw the plane in the trees. We went down to salt water and there was (Mark) walking along, waving at us."

He said that Webber considered the Beaver a total loss, but Easterly arranged for it to be sent to Lake Union and repaired.

Ludwigsen also remembered a more serious crash involving a Transprovincial Grumman Goose operating in Canada.

"We got a call from the State Troopers asking if we could fly them down to Pearse Canal on the border," Ludwigsen said. "The weather was too bad for any flights out of Prince Rupert."

The Grumman, with a pilot and three passengers, had left Stewart BC to return to Prince Rupert and had gone missing. Ludwigsen and the trooper flew down to Tongass Island and up Portland Canal, eventually it ended up in Pearse Canal which was on the Canadian side of the border where they found the Goose, which appeared to have flown directly into Pearse Island in the fog.

"The pilot had survived we heard later," Ludwigsen said. "He was thrown from the wreckage. He managed to crawl into a cedar tree but then he froze to death."

Ludwigsen landed and taxied up to the plane wreckage. They could see the passengers, dead, still trapped in the fuselage. They contacted the Canadians but didn't go ashore because it was Canadian territory.

During that time Ludwigsen further solidified his reputation as the pilot to take people where the "game" was.

"I gained a reputation as a successful hunter and trapper," he said. "I trapped wolves every year in season and the most I ever trapped to be bountied was 28 overall plus nine wolverines trapped."

As chief pilot, Ludwigsen was also responsible to maintaining quality control for Webber Air. He said he didn't like to have to reprimand or fire young pilots but sometimes it was necessary.

"A few didn't take to this very well, but I think I saved a few young pilots' lives just the same," Ludwigsen said in an interview in 1986. "Some don't really know what their limitations were and got too cocky. Some took the attitude that I was getting too old and too cautious but by gosh I'm still flying, whereas a couple of the guys I thought were too stubborn to listen to an 'old and bold' pilot's advice are dead and gone before their time."

Ludwigsen said that he often worked with the airline dispatchers to determine what pilots should take what flights.

"You're sitting around the office with dispatch and the boss like Pete or Jack would say 'don't let him take that one," Ludwigsen said. "You know your pilots, you have a feeling for them, you know that 'he's not that good,' It's just a matter of knowing your people. You sit around talking about bad weather and what to do with people. You talk about what planes they desire, what they feel comfortable with."

Back in Ketchikan, Ludwigsen immediately fell back into familiar flying patterns. One was the constant back and forth to the numerous logging camps. The timber industry was still expanding in the 1960s and more than a dozen remote camps were located in the region, supplying timber to the decade old Ketchikan Pulp Company mill. The mill would operate from 1954 to 1997 and support several thousand jobs in the area.

"The most interesting flying was when we had the Friday afternoon flights to the logging camps," Ludwigsen said. "I was the meanest and ugliest pilot, so I usually took that run! I would tie up at the cook shack and the loggers would clean up and eat dinner. This was a special meal of the week for the guys and the best part was they let the pilot eat with them. It was steak night and sometimes we had prawns too."

He said it was important to be on good terms with the camp cooks. It meant special treats when you pulled into a camp.

"After dinner I would fly a plane load of loggers to Ketchikan," he said. "On Sundays, the flight back would start with yarding the loggers that could talk and walk out of the Fo'c'sle Bar or the Yukon Bar. Both bars were rowdy places when the loggers and fishermen were there. We did not pick up guys from Creek Street where both men and fish went to spawn!"

The Creek Street red light district had officially closed in the mid-1950s, but there was still unofficially "activity" taking place there in the 1960s and early 1970s.

The flights from Ketchikan to Thorne Bay, the largest of the camp, were short – around 15 minutes, but could be very eventful.

"One time, I had a kid named Jim Webster in the co-pilot seat, I was teaching him to fly," Ludwigsen said. "We had a plane load of drunken, rowdy loggers on board and the marijuana smoke was drifting to the cockpit. At that time marijuana was not illegal in Alaska. I have never smoked it, but the second-hand smoke was sure thick on some flights."

Ludwigsen and Webster were flying a Grumman Goose, a large twin engine amphibian plane, that had an open aisle between the two rows of seats. "We heard shouting and clapping and heard funny bumping sounds," he said. "We turned around and a logger had his girlfriend in the aisle between the two sets of bench seats on the walls. They were going at it! Jim turned about six shades of red. I did not know the woman but when we landed all the loggers got out and she flew back to Ketchikan with us, there were no women in camp."

Of course, being back in Southeast Alaska meant that Ludwigsen had to refresh himself with the challenges flying here.

"Bush pilots in Southeast Alaska have one of the most dangerous jobs due to our unpredictable and quick changing weather," he said. "If you are going to land on the water you need to know the signs that indicate the wind velocity. If you see a black streak in the water on a windy day, the wind velocity is 30-60 mph. If the white foam on the top of the waves is picked up and carried the wind velocity is over 60 mph."

Crashes, he said, are just part of the business.

"Sometimes a pilot would take off from a runway and land in the water without retracting his wheels," he said. "That would cause a plane to flip over on its back the fuselage to sink. Other times it would hit a rock or log while taxiing or taking off. Many times, a pilot would push his luck by landing on the water in the dark."

He said that the often-overcast skies and fog puts pilots in a tough position.

"If you use instruments in the clouds with a single engine plane you are stupid as you should be going on VFR (visual flight rules) he said. "Ground flying needs to be visual. Some bush pilots take risks and fly when even the seagulls wouldn't fly. They have mountains named after them."

Otters and Transponders

One of Ludwigsen's most memorable trips in one of the Goose didn't involve human cargo at all.

In more than 50 years of flying throughout Alaska, Ludwigsen carried a remarkable variety of passengers and supplies. But none was more unusual, he says, than the dozens of Aleutian Island sea otters that he released into the waters of Southeast Alaska in the late 1960s in order to help repopulate a local otter population that had died out.

Before the Russians arrived in the late 1700s, it was estimated there were more than 100,000 sea otters in the waters off Alaska. But the otter pelts were worth a fortune in the Far East and they were hunted to near extinction in little more than a century. By 1900, there were sea otters left in a handful of locations in Russia, Alaska, and California. An international treaty introduced a harvest moratorium in 1911, but even that didn't stem the Alaskan decline. By the 1950s, there were no sea otters in Southeast Alaska.

In the mid-1960s, the newly created Alaska Department of Fish and Game began making preparations to transplant some of the remaining Aleutian sea otters to Southeast. The original hope was that they could restore the South East population and then allow residents to have a small yearly harvest to sell some of the furs.

There was also another reason to move some of the vulnerable sea otters from the Aleutians. The federal government had settled on Amchitka Island - half between Dutch Harbor and Adak - as the site for underground nuclear tests. Its remote location figured into testing but also meant that it was one of the few places in the region that had a healthy sea otter population. Scientists were silently concerned that the testing could devastate the otter populations, even though the government was officially announcing that the underground tests would have little or no effect on the marine mammal population. As a result, more than 400 otters were captured at Amchitka, loaded on C-130 transport planes and flown to Southeast, where they were loaded in Grumman Goose and transported to several release sites between 1965 and 1968. Initially otters were released near Yakutat and Sitka, but in 1968, more than 100 were brought to Southern Southeast.

The release sights in 1968 were near Hydaburg where 51 were released and on the Barrier Islands, near the Southwest edge of Prince of Wales Island, near Cape Muzon where 55 were released. Another 50 were released on Cross Sound in northern Southeast.

The Southeast releases were coordinated by Ketchikan based ADFG game biologist Jerry Deppa. A state report on the program quoted Deppa as saying the otters were captured with gillnets in the Amchitka kelp beds and then held in large holding tanks on Amchitka.

"For transport, individual bathtub like kennels were fashioned from galvanized steel approximately 18 inches wide by 36 inches long and 8 inches deep with hinged, perforated, angle iron tops covered by netting," Deppa reported. "The kennels were designed to be stackable and to fit though the rear door of a Grumman Goose amphibious aircraft. They could also hold several inches of water to keep the otter more comfortable."

After the long C-130 flight from Amchitka to the Annette Island airport, the otters were loaded - 10 at a time - into the Grummans which had their seats removed.

"Once the planes landed on the water, the otters were set free one-at-a-time through the plane door by opening the hinged kennel top and letting the animals slide out," Deppa added.

The three Grummans waiting at Annette represented two different airlines. In addition to Ludwigsen flying for Webber Air, Bud Bodding and Ray Renshaw were flying Alaska Airlines Goose. Both Bodding and Renshaw had joined Alaska when it absorbed Alaska Coastal Ellis the year before.

The first batch of otters was taken to the Barrier Islands and then the second batch to Khaz Bay near Sitka. Finally, the three Goose's dropped off 30 more otters in Cross Sound, not far from Glacier Bay.

But once the releasing of sea otters was done in Southeast, Ludwigsen wasn't through with the furry mammals. In October of 1969, nine more otters were to be taken to the Stanley Museum in Vancouver. A ship had been transporting the live otter to the museum, but it broke down in Ketchikan and couldn't continue. Because the otters were specifically for the museum, they could not just be released near Ketchikan.

Ludwigsen the only one willing to make the trip from Ketchikan to Vancouver.

"It was not a nice trip (weatherwise)," Ludwigsen said noting that it was a 4–5-hour trip by Goose. "The otters knew how to talk. Very loud screeching (like eagles) and whistles the whole way down!"

He said it was one of the rare times when the noise of the engines and the radio traffic was good, in that it drowned out the sounds of the sea otters.

It also required a lot of clean up, he said.

"It was pretty smelly in there, and there was a lot of salt-water in the back of the plane," Ludwigsen added.

Ludwigsen said he was supposed to stay in a fairly swanky hotel when he completed the trip, but the hotel employees initially balked because he arrived still smelling of the otters. Eventually, they let him in.

Current estimates are that 26,000 are in Southeast waters, nearly all along the outer islands bordering the Pacific Ocean. With few natural predators and no hunting, they are increasing at a rate of 12-14 percent a year. That increase has sparked concerned that local shellfish numbers are dropping, hurting the lucrative shellfish fisheries in the region.

Moving the otters from Amchitka also proved fortuitous because there was a significant die off of otters after the nuclear tests, according to federal studies.

Ludwigsen made other Goose flights between Southeast Alaska and the Pacific Northwest. On one flight he was heading to Troutdale, Oregon to have work done on the Grumman. The plane was supposed to land on Lake Union near Seattle to clear customs.

"We were supposed to land in Lake Union," Ludwigsen said. "They said 'no you have to go on over to SEATAC (to clear customs).' Oh, gosh, so I went, flew around, called the SEATAC tower 'Grumman 45, need to land and they said okay, we don't have you on the screen, turn your transponder on. I said 'I don't have one. This is an amphib Grumman, not a big Grumman like you think. He said, 'what's your top speed.' '135.' And right behind me was a line of big jets doing 200 and 300 miles an hour. He says 'please get that airplane out of the way. Get down and get the first taxi way off the runway. That taught me a lesson. That could have been a real bad one."

The lack of a transponder on the Grumman Goose also factored into another Ludwigsen trip.

Humanity

"The FAA wanted to charter a Grumman and fly to all the seaplane base stops in Southeast to check them over and make sure that they knew where they were and the locations and the conditions," he said. "We made all the stops, plus a couple of logging camps Pelican, Elfin Cove, all the way clear up to Seward. The FAA guys wanted me to go onto Anchorage. I says 'no, I do not have a transponder and that's a no, no.' So, we went back to Cordova and spent a couple of nights there because of snowstorms."

Another time, Jack Swaim sent Ludwigsen on an unusual trip, taking nine loggers from Ketchikan all the way up to the Malaspina Glacier near Yakutat.

"He said 'there's a small logging camp and a small dirt runway and they want somebody to fly the loggers up there, they need them badly,'" Ludwigsen said. "Ended up with a full plane headed into unknown country, landing on a dirt runway...with potholes and stuff on the runway, you never know. Anyway, we made it, I dropped them off. I took my rifle and stayed one night up in the mountains to try to get a moose. Ended up empty, no moose, flew back home."

After flying dozens of planes over the years, Ludwigsen says that the "045" Goose was always his favorite.

"That airplane, it flew me wherever I wanted," he said. "It did a good job. Even landed on a small lake on Gravina they called Long Lake. I nosed it up to the beach on the lake and went up and was cutting Christmas trees down and some of the Ellis pilots wondered how the hell did I get in there with a Grumman. I went in there twice. But the airplane knew me and I knew her. So, we did good. But she's gone now. Had a bad accident."

Over the years, Ludwigsen truly experienced the wide range of humanity while flying.

At one point, he was tasked with flying a group of US Senators over the area that would become Misty Fjords National Monument in the early 1980s. "We flew from the Unuk River at the Canadian border over Glaciers, Behm Canal, Misty Fjords, Smeaton Bay, Rudyerd Bay and Fitzgibbon Cove," he said. "We flew back and forth for hours as they looked at the rugged scenery. They all appreciated the flight, and I got several letters thanking me for the superb trip."

Another memorable trip was when Ludwigsen was hired to escort Steve Garvey, a former Major League baseball player for a television show about Garvey's Kodak King Salmon Challenge.

"We took his trout fishing seriously," Ludwigsen said. "Had to pack him and his girlfriend to shore because they didn't have boots. Flew him to Waterfall and then they filmed me loading boxes of fish. We landed at a sandy beach in Polk Inlet, and they interviewed me there. We also flew along the cliffs along the west coast of Dall Island."

But, more often than not, the passengers were a little less "high falutin'"

"I mentioned that I was the meanest and ugliest pilot, I did not take any shit from people," he said. "One day a camp manager who ran Thorne Bay with an iron fist was all drunked up. He was a little guy but ornery. He thought he was a big shot, and I was just a pilot so he mouthed off to me. I grabbed him and was going to toss him in the bay, when either Pete or Don stopped me. It would not do for their chief pilot to beat up the head guy from a logging camp, they said. They would lose their business."

He remembered another "eventful" trip, this time to a fishing lodge in Yes Bay.

"I flew in and it was tricky to tie up at the dock as there was a river with a swift current directed at the dock," he said. "I had to tie up on the left side as the (Grumman's) door was on that side and the current would hold me against the dock."

Ludwigsen said the lodge employees were insisting he tie up on the other side of the dock.

"He was angry, and he was feeling his oats that day," Ludwigsen said. "He was cursing me. I tied up on the side I needed to and slid out the pilot's window under the engine to tie up the plane. He was still giving me all kinds of four-letter words. There was a yacht tied up and the people on board were watching."

Ludwigsen said he lost his patience with the dock worker.

"The passengers were off the plane and the guy was still in my face," he said. "I grabbed him and tossed him over the side of the dock. I left him in the water for his friends to fish him out."

Ludwigsen also remembered a "incident" at the Juneau airport.

"There was a big logging conference in Juneau, and I had every big shot from Ketchikan to Anchorage in my Grumman Goose," he said. "By the time we got to Juneau, the weather had socked down, and visibility was poor. I had permission to land and was coming in facing the tower. My wheels were down and locked. I touched down on the wheel on the front of the plane going 60-70 miles per hour and started to brake one side and then the other. Everyone was clapping because the weather was poor, then the tail wheel hit the runway and all the landing gear collapsed, retracting back into the fuselage."

The Goose skidded down the runway on its belly, turning sideways and almost came off the runway before it stopped.

"Everyone was shook up, but all right," Ludwigsen said. "It was getting dark, and the fog was hanging low. I called the tower and told them we had landed on our belly and needed assistance. I stopped the engines and crawled out and opened the doors for the passengers. We all stood outside. Five minutes later, as we stood shivering in the cold November weather, we hear a jet revving its engines. We could not see it, but it was coming our way. Seconds later, an Alaska Airlines jet nosed over us as it took off heading south. The pilot must not have received the information that we had ended up on the runway or else he thought he could make it off the ground before he hit us!"

Ludwigsen said that a mechanic later determined that pressure from the brakes had caused the pins locking the landing gear to break.

"If that had not happened that way (the plane) would have hit the runway going 100 miles an hour with all the wheels retracted," he said. "We looked back on the runway and found the parts of the pins laying there. The story was written in sheer pin parts."

Other than some damage to the "keel" of the plane from skidding on the runway, it was still flyable, and Ludwigsen took it back to Ketchikan the following day.

Eventually, Cessun retired, and Webber Air was sold to Jack Swaim and Max Lukin, logger/pilots from Thorne Bay.

"We continued on the same way, busy, busy, busy," Ludwigsen said. And it was a year-round business, unlike today when nearly all the float plane traffic occurs during the summer flightseeing season.

"In those days, we had winters," Ludwigsen said. "Plenty cold, Coast Guard would break the ice out in Tongass Narrows so we could take airplanes off. Thorne Bay had froze over, they had to get the Coast Guard in there to bust up the ice to get people out. Whale Pass was the same way, but a little more open to the wind and I had a trip into Whale Pass to get some passengers. I had to land about a mile or so from the camp and taxi really slow, breaking ice as I went, making sure that I didn't start gouging, tearing stuff off the airplane. I made it to the camp. Once I got that done, they went out with their boom boat and broke up the ice and opened it up for my takeoff."

One day, he said, Webber received an usual request.

"We had a call from Sinclair Logging, they wanted Dr. Wilson to fly out to the camp for an emergency," he said "Nowadays, and even them days, Doctors don't come running down and jump in an airplane and fly off somewhere out in the boonies. But Dr. Wilson was a nice gentleman. I took him to Cholmondeley where the camp was. He examined the patient, put him on a stretcher and, as we took off, Dr. Wilson kept on him. We landed in Ketchikan (about 20 minutes later), but he had died in the airplane while we were flying."

Ludwigsen would stay with Webber until a major tragedy hit the company in 1978.

Jack Swaim and 11 passengers died when Grumman Goose 045 crashed into the water off Prince of Wales Island shortly after leaving the Labouchere Bay logging camp at the north end of the island. It was the largest loss of life in a Grumman Goose crash at the time and proved to be the undoing of Webber Airlines.

"He was seen by some loggers working a clear cut on a side hill," Ludwigsen said. "They saw him above the mist and then he disappeared. The sounds of the airplane changed. They thought the plane went down."

Ludwigsen was on a flight back from Hyder when Webber contacted him to search for the missing Goose.

"They had me come in and switch to a Cessna 185 for the search," he said. "By the time I got there the fog had disappeared. In the tide rips were life jackets and plane parts. The vacuum tank of the plane had been crushed lengthwise, like the nose had hit the surface of the water going at a high speed."

The National Transportation Safety Board never reached a conclusion on what brought the plane down, primarily because the wreckage – and most of the bodies – ended up unrecoverable, 1,200 feet deep in Sumner Strait.

The NTSB report surmised that the plane had been overloaded because it was only rated to carry 11 people, including the pilot. There was also evidence that cargo had been added at Lab Bay that further overloaded the plane.

Besides losing his friend, Ludwigsen lost his favorite airplane.

He believes that the large amount of medications Swaim was taking for his heart trouble was also a factor in the crash. Another factor could have been that Swain was under pressure to get the passengers to Ketchikan in a hurry.

After the tragic accident killed the owner of Webber Air and destroyed Grumman 045, the Swaim family decided to sell Webber's assets to Flair Air, which was run by a pilot that Ludwigsen didn't like.

"One evening as we were all sitting around waiting for good or bad news," he said. "When Marilyn (Swaim) got up and said we were selling, I stood up and said I quit. I didn't like the gentlemen. Other pilots also quit. I went to work on a pile driver, did some work on buildings to keep money in the bank."

Before long, Ludwigsen got a call from Kirk Thomas at Tyee Air and went to work as that airline's chief pilot.

"It was the same as Webber, we were busy, busy," Ludwigsen said.

The timber industry was not booming like it had in 1960s and early 1970s, but it was still very vibrant. There were also major regional infrastructure projects like the Swan Lake hydro project that kept things at Tyee hopping.

But then history repeated itself. Webber, now called SEA Air, bought out Tyee. "I just walked out the door and said, 'thank you,'" Ludwigsen said.

Once again, Ludwigsen was not out of flying work for very long. He was contacted by Bob Berto at Southeast Stevedoring about being the company's corporate pilot.

"I was a corporate pilot, required at least 18 hours a day on the job," he said. "That was a good job, nice pay. Met log ships with sea pilots and immigration officials."

With Southeast Stevedoring, he originally flew a Cessna 206 amphibian, but never much liked that plane.

"When I was pre-flighting the 206 at Annette, I found that the floats had damaged the keel, consequently 206 was flown back to Kansas for repairs and to the replace the floats," Ludwigsen said.

But then the company acquired a DeHavilland Beaver from the Bell Island resort.

"It was a beautiful, cherry airplane from the Border Patrol in Texas," he said. "Flew that plane everywhere. I loved it! Took that Beaver from one end of Southeast to the other."

He often made company trips to Prince Rupert.

"Rupert trips were nice," he said. "There was a big flower shop. I'd bring home an airplane full of flowers. Bought for $18 in Rupert for myself."

Ludwigsen said he would occasionally fly Stevedoring personnel for non-business reasons.

"One of the stockholders in Southeast Stevedoring had a big yacht and permission from the Canadians to fish off Langara Island (in the Haida Gwaii)," Ludwigsen said. "Ricky Smith would give them information on the fish that he caught. He called me a couple of times to come over and pick up stuff, it's quite a flight." Ludwigsen said he had to fly to Prince Rupert first to clear customs and then out to Graham Island and Langara. One time they were met by the Royal Canadian Mounted Police.

"The Mounties stopped us from loading, the people on the island were complaining that no local guides had been used to help fish," Ludwigsen said. "People like you or me can't fish without a guide. We showed them some paperwork that came from the Canadian government. (the locals) weren't too happy. They were losing money."

Flying back, over the several fishing boats, Ludwigsen noticed that the fishermen were giving him "the finger."

"They didn't like Americans out there,' he said. "But it ended up fine, Ricky Smith got his fish."

Another unusual duty was one that local residents asked him to do four times, to airdrop the ashes of loved ones on locales that were important to them in life.

He dropped his sister Helen's ashes on Deer Mountain. He dropped the ashes of Ruth LeMay over Coffman Cove. He dropped the ashes of Violet Hansen at Loring. And dropped the ashes of longtime fisherman Nels Nelson at Dall Head on Gravina Island.

Hung Up His Wings

After more than a decade with Southeast Stevedoring, Ludwigsen retired in 1998 and moved to Wrangell, where he and Ann could be closer to his son, Manny, and his grandchildren.

Ludwigsen retired from flying from Southeast Stevedoring in 1998. It was also the year he quit flying. He said he stopped flying and "never had an inkling to do it again."

"I had enough to do around the house (in Wrangell) to keep busy," he said. "Sewers, powerlines, lots to do."

But there was another reason why he quit flying after more than half a century.

"Eyeballs," he said. "I couldn't pass the flight physical. I couldn't even pass a driver's test. Southeast Stevedoring wanted me to stay for sure but that was it. I knew that you couldn't start fooling around with bad eyes, trying to cheat a little bit, you can't fake it."

He was 72 when he stopped flying, more than two decades ago.

"Finally, one day, Herman said: 'Ann, I'm making small mistakes, I can't do it anymore," So, we moved to Wrangell.

"Our grand kids were growing up and we wanted to be there with them," Herman said. "We bought a nice set of beach properties south of town, about eleven miles south on the (Zimovia) highway. A beautiful spot. Manny had half of it, and we had half."

The Ludwigsen's put a "manufactured" house on their half of the property. But Ludwigsen did a lot of personalizing on the house.

"I ordered my own stuff," he said. "Like two by six studs, three quarter inch plumbing, and rebuilt the house. They had the front of the house looking backwards toward the trees. It cost me $2,500 bucks just to redo the (designs) so we could see the beach. It was built up to our specifications."

Beating the Odds

For a while, Ludwigsen helped his son build floats, but for the most part he settled into retirement, for as long as his body held out.

"I continued to fish and hunt as long as I could get around but the diabetes," he said. "I could get around okay, but I couldn't get into the woods."

Diabetes would eventually claim both his lower legs. Then he got bladder cancer. They had been in Wrangell a couple of years.

"Herman wasn't feeling well, and he had gout," Ann said.

They went to Seattle for tests.

"The doctor (in Seattle) said you have cancer, and you have six months," Herman said. That was in 2001. They stayed at Fred Angerman's apartment in Seattle while undergoing treatment.

"The doctor said 'Herman, it's really bad but we have one treatment,'" Herman said. "You have to go home and lay on a bed with a big tube and you drink this stuff (medicine) and you wiggle around all night and this killed it (the cancer)! He said, 'you're lucky.' "
"It's gone," he continued "And it's been almost 20 years."

Ludwigsen also survived prostate cancer.

"The doctor in Seattle said, 'when we treat people for prostate cancer, we have a limit of how far we can go," Ludwigsen said. "You're on number nine and on ten you won't make it. You're right at the edge, we'll give it our best shot."

Ludwigsen said his prostate was heavily radiated.

"But it did it," he said. "The radiation seeds are still in there; the doctors see them when they x-ray me."

Ludwigsen has also undergone three hip replacements.

"The left one kept falling out," he said. "So, the doctor had to replace the original hip replacement. But then the right one went to hell."

He said it fell apart before he had quit flying. They were on a visit to Wrangell.

"That fell apart on Christmas Eve," he said. "I took a shower, it got hot, walked down a set of stairs, sat in a chair. And then plunk, the hip just slipped right out. Talk about pain! They had to call my doctor in Seattle and ask him how in the hell to put Herman back together. The doctors said, 'what do you have up there to stretch him out with?' That's what they do, stretch your muscles.
Tim Buness, my son Manny and three or four other guys pulled me apart. I was wide awake, laying there watching them."

Then, Ludwigsen said, they took him into where the x-ray machine was to see whether the hip was back in place, but it wasn't.

"So, they went back again and pulled me apart and stretched me," he said. "They fought that for hours but finally got it into place. But I've been pretty lucky on that medical stuff."
"A lot of bad things have happened," he added. "But everything is fine now."

Ludwigsen said that Wrangell proved to be a "mannish" town. "Lots of hunting, fishing, trips up the Stikine river," he said." Lots of logging roads to drive on."

But, he noted, it wasn't necessarily a good place for Ann because like many small towns it's always a challenge to fit in if you are not "from there." "They didn't even know Herman was a pilot!" Ann said. "I got really mad."

Eventually as the grandkids grew up, they felt less of a reason to stay in Wrangell. They moved back to Ketchikan 2013.

So why Ketchikan?

"We still knew a lot of people here," Anita said. "I practically grew up here"

Ludwigsen's oldest daughter Lynn lives with her family in Southern California, his son Manny lives in Ketchikan, and his youngest daughter Jocelyn lives in Chicago.

Lynn worked for Verizon, the City of Long Beach, and also owned a Bed and Breakfast and wedding venue in Colorado. Manny worked in the transportation industry for 41 years. Jocelyn worked in 13 countries for 12 years as a Technical Trainer and Project Manager for ConAgra, IBM, Wrigley's, and Mars before she retired due to disability. Lynn has three daughters, Manny has three daughters and one son, and Jocelyn has four stepsons.

These days, the Ludwigsen's are watching with great pride as their oldest grandson, Max, is beginning his career as a float plane pilot. He recently got his float plane rating and is hoping to work for one of the local companies.

The Ludwigsen's live in the Pioneer Heights development near Wolf Point. It gives them a view of the airport and of the jets flying into and out of Ketchikan.

Ludwigsen enjoys seeing the planes come and go and also the numerous float planes that leave the airport seaplane dock.

They like the fact that deer and bear wander onto their property now and again.

"A couple of times a black bear walked right by here and looked in the windows, him and I were eyeball to eyeball," Herman said. "I got right up close to the window and he could just stare at me."

Unfortunately, Ludwigsen's pilots eye spots things that worry him when he watches float planes take off the water, especially the Beavers.

"I'm afraid they are going to crash sometimes," he said. "The pilots come out of other places. We know they have six or seven passengers, and they have a pretty heavy fuel load, and they get up off the water about a hundred feet and they make some very, very sharp turns. Scares the hell of out me."

Primarily because Ludwigsen knows that you have to be careful with Beavers on takeoff because the fuel intakes on the tanks are near the front and the fuel can pool up near the back cutting the engine off sometimes, causing the plane to stall if the pilot is not expecting it.

He said the newer planes have fuel injection which alleviates the problem.

"A couple of times, Pete, he wasn't too sure about me because I was too gung-ho, a crazy kid trying to fly," Ludwigsen said. "But he settled down about me. I buzzed a boat one day and he heard about it. He didn't like that."

How close did Ludwigsen come to the boat.

"Well, I didn't' hit the trolling poles!" he noted.

He is less sure about his final flight in 1998.

"It was in the Beaver for Southeast Stevedoring, it was a short flight, I was sent somewhere," he said. "It was probably Chomly because Jim Taro had a bunch of business there in those days. I remember it was short trip. Just brought the plane back and put it in the hangar at Peninsula Point, wished it well."

He said he remembers feeling relieved.

"I felt like I was saved," he said. "I was getting tired, and I just felt relieved. I went out to my house at Waterfall and thought 'I'm home.' "

Herman, FAA, and the Wright Brothers

No, at 93, Herman Ludwigsen is not old enough to have flown with the Wright Brothers! But on Sept. 11, 2020, the Federal Aviation Administration awarded him with the national Wright Brother's Master Pilot Award, an award given only to pilots who have 50 years of total flight time and have contributed to the safety of flying.

The COVID 19 pandemic limited the attendance at the ceremony at the Tongass Historical Museum to 20 close friends, but – as FAA administrator Lana Boler noted – the room included local pilots with well over 100,000 flight hours, **not counting** Ludwigsen's 32,000.

Ludwigsen's grandson Max nominated him for the award and worked with the FAA to make it happen. Three longtime Ketchikan pilots also lent their support to Ludwigsen getting the award.
"Herman is a legend in Ketchikan," Jeff Carlin of Carlin Aviation wrote in a nomination letter to the FAA, adding that he had known Ludwigsen since 1975. "I worked with Herman as a dock boy. He trained me to be a pilot and was my mentor for many

years. Herman was the man that everyone wanted to work with, be trained by and emulate. I cannot think of anyone more deserving."

Mike Cessnun – who also started out working as a dock boy for Ludwigsen and went on to be a jet pilot for Alaska Airlines – called Ludwigsen "one of my true heroes" and "a larger-than-life figure."

"Herman had an instinct and a knowledge of flying in Alaska that was a rare gift," Cessnun wrote to the FAA. "He made a practice of taking flights when the weather was marginal and the destination difficult...he was truly the best for these flights. He had a knack of helping you learn not just so you could be a better pilot but to keep you alive. During my time at Alaska Airlines, I came in contact with a number of pilots that credited Herman with teaching them important flying lessons."

Kirk Thomas also noted that he had known Ludwigsen since the early 1970s. Thomas also employed Ludwigsen for a time at Tyee Air.

"I have worked with well over a hundred pilots during my long aviation career in Ketchikan and without exception we all look to Herman Ludwigsen as the example we want to follow," Thomas wrote in his letter of support to the FAA. "It was not unusual for him to take me or one of the other pilots aside and talk to us about something of concern he saw in our flying habits or skills. He is an outstanding individual...and is respected and is a legend in the Ketchikan Aviation Community."

During the ceremony, Boler also presented a pin to Ann Ludwigsen in recognition of the fact that no pilot is successful without the support of his family. She was delighted to receive it.

After the ceremony, Herman received a letter from US Senator Lisa Murkowski – who had flown with Ludwigsen in the past. The Murkowski family frequently flew to Mirror Lake south of Ketchikan with Herman.

"Your contributions are one of the many reasons Alaska is such a wonderful place to live and raise a family," Murkowski wrote. "This is a tremendous accomplishment as you are now recognized as one of Alaska's flight pioneers."

Aviation timeline provided by the FAA

Feb. 2, 1948 – Made application and received Student Pilot Certificate #886824

Mar. 3, 1948 – First official Solo Flight in a Luscombe Silvaire to gain his single engine seaplane rating.

April 10, 1948 – Received his private pilot's license after recommendation from flight instructor Edwin Cessnun of Webber Air Service and recommended by examiner James Webber.

1950-1955 – Private pilot time flying to hunt and fish.

July 7, 1955 – Passed his commercial pilot written exam at Merrill Aviation at Boeing Field in Seattle.

May 28, 1956 – Passed the written test for an instrument rating.

June 2, 1956 – Received his multi-engine land rating in a Cessna 140, N1137D, reporting total PIC time of 1,200 hours.

June 5, 1956 – Received his multi-engine land and sea rating in a Grumman G44 Widgeon, N67586.

June 5, 1956 – Received his instrument rating in a Cessna 140, N76439.
1956 – Wien Airlines, Pilot in C46, 55 hours

1956-1962 – Bethel Charter Pilot, acquiring approximately 5,500 hours

1960 – Shell Oil Charter pilot flying on the North Slope acquiring 285 hours

1963-1966 – Northern Consolidated Captain, acquiring 2,302 hours

1967 – 1977 – Webber Air, chief pilot, acquiring 21,367 hours

1979-1981 – Tyee Airlines, pilot, acquiring 1,830 flight hours

1983-1998 – Southeast Stevedoring, pilot

Total flight time logged: 32,405 hours

Trapper/Hunter

In May of 2001, Herman Ludwigsen sat down with a representative of the Alaska Trapping Hall of Fame and talked about his decades of experience in the Alaskan wilderness.

"In those days we'd run our own trap lines with airplanes," he said. "Had a good time trapping mink, marten, a few otters. Chased a few wolves out on the frozen lakes of Southeast. Did the things we thought was right. We'd shoot a seal when it was legal and drop it from the air, cut it loose from the pontoon and while we were flying by an open lake, we'd let it splatter. The wolves, in a week or ten days, a cycle in which they run, would come by and we would fire one or two shots from the plane. Never did get one but we had a lot of fun doing it."

Later the state of Alaska banned hunting wolves from planes, except when done by the state to specifically cull packs. Later it was also made it illegal to hunt wolves on the same day as flying into a location.

At one point, Ludwigsen said he had more than 50 wolf traps. Wolf trapping was especially lucrative because not only was the pelt valuable, but the state of Alaska had a $50 bounty on wolves.

"We'd shoot seals and flew out to these different inlets and bays," he said. "We'd make wolf sets in saltwater. The wolves would then come to the beach. We did pretty good. There were two or three guys in Ketchikan that did that. I'm still upset (with the State). They owed me money for wolf bounties and never paid. They ran out of money, they said, and just wouldn't pay me. We did a little otter trapping. When we had the wolf traps out, I'd run up on the brush a ways and set a few marten sets. Never bothered with the mink because the prices weren't good enough. We had good marten there, especially on Prince of Wales Island."

He followed a specific pattern in his wolf sets.

"We'd make them just about 3/4 tide on the high tide mark where the water would come over and cover your set and wash the human scent away," he said. "Your footprints would be there, but we would make a three-trap set with a pyramid of rocks out in the pool that was usually in about 6-8 inches of water. We'd anchor the trap with a long chain with a piece of heavy driftwood, something that would look natural to the beach and staple that to it. When the wolf got in there, he would get in and then back out and take this wood drag which was fairly good sized. Sometimes we cut down alder; but it had to look natural. He would take it up the beach a ways and he'd get caught. We'd pop him with a .22 magnum. It was a lighter rifle."

He always used seal meat for bait.

"The rottener the better," he said. "I'd have a weak stomach when it came to that stuff. We'd have it in a barrel, and we'd reach in with a gaff hook and bring it out and put it in a gunny sack and tie it to the floats on the airplanes. Boy that stunk!" Ludwigsen said it was important to put a heavy rock over the bait, so the wolf couldn't easily get at the seal meat.

"But then he would work around it "he said. "You find these little dinky rocks with seaweed growing on it, smaller than your hand. Set them all around the traps where the seaweed would float, and the wolf can't see that trap. Can't see any iron at all. The seaweed camouflages it".

He said he primarily used a "114" trap.

"The seal meat was so rotten, there was plenty of eagles looking at it. The smell and the juice formed in a little pool of water and it would make a little trail or creek down to the lower part of the tide level," he said. "And if a wolf was running on the beach by the timberline, he'd smell that trickle in the salt water and he would follow that to your set."

There was also a specific direction for the trap to face.

"Your set always had to be facing so the wolf would come into your set with three traps on a triangular shape towards the pyramid," he said. "It had to be facing the woods. They don't like to come down the beach and walk into the set with their back to the woods. They want to be able to see their escape route."

He said that marten sets were a little different.

"With the marten sets they would smell the seal," Ludwigsen said. "We would take seal blubber and nail it to the tree. We'd make our marten set on a lean pole. I think 90 percent of trappers would use a leaner going up to a tree, so the marten has a little trail to run up to it. Then about two or three feet above that we'd staple or nail some seal blubber or meat, or duck feathers. If it was a legal duck you could use it for that. Also, I've never done it, but you can use squirrel or other ducks like the Merganser and burn the feathers. The smell attracts marten from long distance. I've had marten come to the sets of mine where I rub the seal juice on the tree, and they eat the bark. They think that's good eatin'."

Ludwigsen estimates that over the years he trapped more than 28 wolves.

Sometimes he tried to use methods besides traps.

"I was flying a 185 for Webber going up toward Whale Pass and I had a woman passenger in the airplane," he said. "We were flying over a salt chuck and I saw a wolf swimming across, I didn't have a gun. I landed the airplane and taxied up along that wolf in the water and I grabbed an axe and I hit that sucker right in the head. I popped him real good, it's a wonder I didn't chop a hole in the float. So, he got to the beach and started running up the beach. I ran the airplane up on the beach and hollered to the woman that I would be right back. And I grabbed that axe and went into the woods after that damned wolf, but I never found it. She thought I was nuts. She wanted out of the airplane. I don't blame her."

He also trapped wolverine occasionally, using something called "chad and cheese" for bait. "God that was good stuff," he said. "Humungous smell though. That was something".

Ludwigsen said that although wolverine pelt brought good prices, they were harder to trap and very hard to deal with once they were trapped, even more challenging than otter.

"I used a 330 Conovaire trap (for wolverine)," he said. "Right in the back of the cubby, a good-sized log leaning out, right next to the salt water. Right down tight. Put a couple of rocks around the cubby so he couldn't go through the sides and then install this 330 right in front of the hole and cover it with a little moss and around the edges and on the two triggers that stick down. There are two fingers about six inch, fingers that trip the set. We'd go up on the beach and find this hollow grass and stick this grass on the two triggers. You'd leave a bit of camouflage; it was wintertime, and it was dry, but it made a damn good set. Worked real good got nine wolverines that way."

Ludwigsen remembered a "battle" with a particularly wily wolverine up in Misty Fjords.

"I had one in Rudyerd Bay, he's still there by all means," Ludwigsen said. "He knew me, and I knew him, and he knew exactly what he was doing. Every time he came through my trap, he'd spring it. I don't know how, he'd get the bait, come out of the set and he left his calling card, droppings, always right by the set. So, I tried to get as smart as I could, and I got a jump trap, an Oneida jump trap. I boiled it in hemlock juice and wore gloves and never touched it with human hands. I put this Oneida jump right in front of the 330 trap and I put it in a plastic bag so it wouldn't freeze into the ground. I buried it down to the ground just below the entrance and mossed it up as much as I could. You couldn't tell it was there, but he knew it. He'd spring that sucker first. I just never got him. This bugger was smart! To this day, I'm glad I didn't get him, but I would like to have."

Wolverine pelts always fetched good prices; one was particularly profitable to Ludwigsen.

"I traded one, a nice big one, to Tongass Trading Company for a Blaze King wood stove," he said. The stove was over $900. They got the wolverine."

One of Ludwigsen's favorite places to trap was in Cholmondeley Sound on Prince of Wales Island. Locals call the place "Chomly."

"Back in 1948, I went with my brother Arnold on our trolling boat over to Chomly where Norman Olson and his wife Harriet lived," he said. "We anchored in the small harbor at Babe Island. I was just a young fellow and that was an adventure, going out and trapping in the middle of winter. Arnold and I had a lot of mink traps. We didn't try for otter in those days, they were tough. Tough to skin, tough to stretch, tough to turn and the mink and marten were so much easier that it was a lot better. And the prices weren't bad in them days."

One early November, they were tied up in Chomley waiting for the trapping season to start.

"This boat comes in, low, green ugly looking boat, like a fish pirate boat would look!" Ludwigsen said. "This guy was a poacher, and he was smart. His name was Rastus Brown on the Islander. He had Fish and Game fooled and they could never catch him. He would trap (out of season) and send the pelts to Canada. He was going down to the Nass River and selling them and making good money."

Ludwigsen said that he and his brother were successful trapping together.

"We, of course, had beach runs with a skiff and a 10-horse kicker usually," he said. "We had 100 mink one season. Just living with Norman and Harriet on our boats. We'd get a couple of mallards and a goose and have our Thanksgiving dinner. This was before (Norman and Harriet) built their home and boat works there. There were other fellows in the area trapping like Del Richardson. We each had our own areas and we put out trapline signs (everyone else) left you alone."

But there were a few trappers who used illegal means.

"You could hear them at night, pit lighting," he said. "They were shooting mink. You can call them up when you roll along the beach at night, I've done this, but I didn't shoot any. You can see the minks little green eyes running along the beach and you could squeak your lips like you were calling a dog and they'd come right to you. And you could pop them using a .410 shotgun and it wouldn't hurt (the pelts) too bad. Yeah, we could hear those guys."

He said the fur buyers were aware of the illegal trapping, but there were ways to get around detection.

"You dry it on your stretcher boards, and you turn it before it gets too stiff and turn the fur side out," he said. "They would wash it in Felsatna soap, and it would dissolve the blood and sort of close up the holes."

He said one particular buyer, Norm Goldberg, was very careful when buying pelts.

"Everybody knew when Goldberg would be in town and he'd stay at one of the local hotels and people would bring their pelts and big gunny sacks of dried fur," Ludwigsen said. "Some of them had them in bags or on strings and they'd bring them through the hotel right up into the lobby and then to Goldberg's room and lay them out there."

Besides wolverine, Ludwigsen said that otter was the toughest to trap.

"If you have a coil of rope on the dock or the float an otter will come and poop on it," Ludwigsen said. "He'll go right there and leave his droppings there. So, we got smart and used poop chutes. Up on the otter slides you can see, usually on a point, where they are working around, the otter will work a point and slide down into the water between the rocks. You can get up inside the timber and you can see where he's been sliding. He's sliding on his belly. They are sliding and scooting down but once they get to the log he's got to stop and step over it, that's where you put your set. And if that doesn't work and he comes to an area where it's a little more level, they usually level the ground, it looks like a dinky park. They level it down and you find all their poop. You had to be careful carrying that away and cut a hole there and put your trap down there. And then put poop over it."

Then as the otter were pooping again on the spot they would step on the trap.
Ludwigsen said that he had respect for the game wardens who were tasked with catching poachers in the area.

"One was Dan Ralston, a real nice gentleman of a guy," he said. "He was a hard one. He wanted to catch people. He had an assistant, Johnny Windler, another real tough guy. They would snowshoe across Chomly from one bay to another trying to catch us or the Islander. They were tough, old time game wardens and they knew how to catch people. We tried not to break the law. They were good game wardens, honest, didn't try to lie or entrap you into anything. If they caught you on your boat skinning, or catch a beaver out of season, they take you. If you were honest enough and faithful enough, they would come on the boat and have coffee. Another guy named Frank Sharp, he was from Angoon or Hoonah. He was the toughest of the tough. He wanted everyone that was trapping or shooting deer to go to jail because you were breaking the law, and maybe we were!"

Besides trapping, Ludwigsen also spent a lot of time hunting deer in the mountains of Southern Southeast Alaska. He remembered a few of the trips.

"Terry Wills dropped me off on a high lake and I had my tent and throw-away sleeping bag and stove," Ludwigsen said. "I walked from the lake up into the high country. It was a beautiful night and a beautiful morning. I woke up and ate a few crackers, then I shot two nice bucks. They were really nice big guys; the limit was four and I was crazy. So, I got the two dressed out and started dragging them one at a time with my pack on my back, dragging them down to the lake below where I was supposed to be picked up." He said the ravine was about 1,500 feet lower than where he shot the deer.

"I could get the deer down easier that way," he said. "So, I went back up and shot two more. So, I had four big deer down."

But then the weather started to change.

"When you're a pilot like I had been for many years, you notice that sky turns and pretty soon you know how a Southeaster is, you don't wait too long, you need to get in and get out or you're gonna be stuck," he said. "So, I got these four deer down the ravine, I got them down to the lake and still had my tent and a little bit of junk to eat. I sat there on the edge of the lake and it was just getting close to dark, and it started to rain, and the fog set in."

By then Wills had come back to retrieve him.

"There I was I could hear the airplane, circling around," Ludwigsen said. "But he couldn't land, couldn't get in there."

It got dark and Ludwigsen pitched his tent on the hillside and crawled into his sleeping bag to wait out the weather.

"I shivered and shook, all night long," he said. "I didn't have much to eat, I had a little fire going, Ann had made stew, it was in a little plastic jug. I had some of that. It helped but it was plenty wet, and I didn't have a raincoat. I had plastic bags, so I cut one out and stuck my head through it, I was able to keep my body fairly dry."

When the sun came up the weather was same, Ludwigsen said. Rotten.

"I hung the (four) deer up and took a deer heart and liver in my pocket and packed up my junk and went back up the mountain," he said. "I figured that the only way I would get out of there was to go back up the damn mountain and go down the other side to saltwater. It was pretty steep with slides. I got down to saltwater, but now the searchers didn't know where I was. You make a mistake. You are not at the lake. Where the hell are you?"

He made another camping spot, under a large cedar.

"I almost made a fatal mistake," he said. "I had a can of sterno which helps start fires. I had a pack of matches. There were about eight matches in that little can and every one of them wouldn't light but one because they got damp from alcohol. Bad mistake. Bad mistake. I got the one match going and I lit that can of sterno and I got some cedar from the side of an old rotten tree and I spent the night there. It was raining and blowing like all get out. I knew I was on saltwater and could get clams and mussels down there to eat. As long as I kept the fire going, I was fine. They found me the next day. I could see them flying around, I got out on the edge of the saltwater and I was throwing rocks out in the water to make a wake. The searchers knew it couldn't be ducks splashing in the water, so they made a low pass and saw me standing on the beach."

Unfortunately, by then, he said, the deer carcasses had gone bad, so the hunting trip was a complete waste.

While he was in Bethel, Ludwigsen said he enjoyed moose hunts around the Inoko River.

"We saw a nice big bull back in the swamp behind one of the sloughs we landed in," he said. "He was a fair-sized animal; he wasn't a baby. It was close to rutting season too. I had a .33 Winchester with me, which is a good killing rifle. We got in the brush there where the moose was and lo and behold that moose came right after me. We went around a big old spruce tree three times. He was serious, he was going after me. He didn't think that I should be there. This went on for a while, but I finally popped him. He was a beautiful animal, but he wanted to take me. He knew he had some lovin' to do and I was in his way!"

Ludwigsen said that the area near the Innoko was a popular place to take hunters in those days.

"In them days, it was pretty cheap. We figured a couple of hundred dollars to take a guy up and shoot a moose and be home the same afternoon."

He said that sometimes he saw moose that needed to be preserved.

"On one of my trips I ran into an almost pure white bull" he said. "Beautiful guy. And I got awfully close to him. The only brown on him was right down the center of his backbone, started at the back of his neck down to his tail and the rest was white, pure white and beautiful. But I didn't want to kill him. I got back to Bethel and called (zoos) down in the states. I called three different outfits about this white animal we could tranquilize and get him and have him on display. They said they didn't deal in 'freaks.' I think they made a bad mistake."

Of course, there were also plenty of bear in the mountains of Southeast as well, although Ludwigsen conceded, after his first bear hunt, he wasn't that interested in chasing them.

"We went up with the Super Cub and I landed there in Lake Creek and walked up the stream," he said. "I wanted a bear; I wanted a bear bad, a big grizzly. That was before we needed tags and everything else. I had my .33 Winchester. I was walking up the brush and there sure enough was a nice big Chocolate brown grizzly. This guy had a hump on his back, and he was trying to get some dog salmon out of the creek. He saw me and I saw him. He didn't survive. I shot him twice with the .33 right behind the ear and he dropped. He just laid there. That was my first big bear. I still had three or four more shells and I walked up to him. He was just laying there in a big brown heap. People use a stick to poke them to make sure they ain't gonna come up and take you. I went up and hit him with the barrel of my rifle. And you'll never believe what happened. My gun fell apart! The magazine was spring loaded with two little screws under the barrel that vibrated out. When I hit the bear with the rifle, all my shells and springs (came out) right there in front of me. I said a few words. But he didn't move."

Ludwigsen skinned the bear by himself, not an easy task. He fleshed the bear out, cleaned him, loaded him into the Super Cub and brought him back to Ketchikan.

"I did all the hard work once I got home," he said. "I stretched him out, and finished him, the ears, the lips, and the paws right down to the last knuckles like you do with a marten or a mink," Ludwigsen said. "Got him all cleaned up and had him tanned."

After his retirement from flying, when Ludwigsen moved to Wrangell, he continued to hunt and fish with his son and grandchildren.

"That was the legacy from me teaching my son how to fish and hunt with our little boat he said. "He got it into his granddaughters that they have to do something in the woods. They drive their four wheelers and go up with him. They parked their trucks on the logging roads, they get out and walk when they can't drive. These girls are good! They are right in there cleaning the deer and packing it. They're up in my deer hanging shed, wrapping, and cutting the meat. Now we have a grandson who is 16 months old and we are really going to get to that kid."

Nearly two decades later, Ludwigsen's grandson, Max, is following in his flying footsteps, training to become a commercial pilot and also following Herman as an outdoorsman.

"I've lived my whole life in the air or the woods," Herman Ludwigsen said. "That's why I don't like the States. If I go to Seattle for three days, it's too long. I don't drive. I have to take a taxicab. I don't like that country. I feel more at home on the beach or if I can go walk out in the brush. My dad was a boat builder, and we didn't have much money in the thirties and forties. I'd get a lot of deer; we'd catch a lot of fish and halibut. Same thing when we lived in Bethel, we lived on moose meat, king salmon and ptarmigan. Had a lot of rabbits, but I don't like to eat rabbits though. Really nice, but that's been my whole life. I would never trade it for anybody else. There are so many people now that have to spend thousands and thousands of dollars for what I did most of my life."

Although, he conceded, there have been a few times when his outdoor life could have been the end of him.

"I went down to Boca de Quadra," he said. "One of the long arms, they called it Mink Arm. I was making a wolf set there and I had the Super Cub about a mile away from where I was making the set way up in the flats. I was almost done when I heard wolves howl on one side of a steep ravine in the valley. I could hear wolves on one side and someone barking and howling on the other side. They were talking back and forth. I howled because I was good at that. I'd howl and they'd bark, and I'd howl, and bark and it went on for 10 to 20 minutes."

After a while, Ludwigsen decided he might be able to bag a couple of the wolves for a bounty.

"So, I went out to the middle of the mudflats and I down into a little hole in the muck and I hunkered down," he said. "All of a sudden, silence, and I thought 'wow,' wondering what's happening. When you are laying there in the mud and you get to thinking that somebody is watching you and I slowly turn around to look behind me and here comes seven or eight wolves on the dead run and they are less than 100 feet from me. There was slime coming out of their mouths and their tongues were hanging out and they were running like all get out. Hell, they were right on me! I thought I was dead. I thought this is the end of it."

Ludwigsen grabbed his rifle and began shooting. And missed every shot.

"I never hit one," he said. "And they went right on (past). There were blacks and oranges, beautiful wolves, all around me on both sides and they went up the hill on the other side. I never hit one. Looking at them, that was close. It took me a while to get back to the airplane to get home. I was pale as a ghost."
 He was still shaking when he got home.

"Ann asked me, 'how come you're so damned white?'"

The Planes

Over his half century in the air, Ludwigsen flew on a variety to types of airplane. Naturally, he has some thoughts about them.

Grumman Goose

There is little question that the Grumman Goose, especially one he fondly calls "045" was one of his favorite planes.

"We just fit," he said. "It just knew what I wanted to do, and it did it. It did its work very well."

Pilots often say that flying a Cessna 185 is like driving a sports car and that flying a DE Havilland Beaver is like driving a bus. Ludwigsen said flying a Goose was like driving a train. Big and powerful. Its' twin 450 horsepower Pratt and Whitney engines meant it could go from one end of Southeast to the other in three or four hours. The Goose had a cruising speed of 145 mph and a range of 640 miles, almost enough to fly from Ketchikan to Seattle without refueling.

"Once you got it going, it just went straight," he said. "It carried a tremendous load. As big as it is, it looks clumsy, but you can do whatever you want with it."

He called the Goose a very stable airplane and safe to fly.

Ludwigsen said that he occasionally did things with the Goose that the Ellis pilots' thought were "crazy."

"That was in rough weather sometimes, " he said."They weren't nice days, but they didn't seem bad to me. The airplane handled it fine."

He said the sheer weight of the Goose made him confident that it could handle more severe weather than smaller planes.
"The float planes, the 185, the Beaver, with pontoons, they take a hammering in bad weather," he said. "It doesn't really hurt them, but it loosens the rivets in the floats."

He said it helps to have knowledge of the weather.

"Some of it was because I was a fisherman earlier," he said. "And I got used to really bad weather. It's just a matter of experience. Not saying I am the best in the world at experience, but I had some and it paid off."

The Grumman Goose (they don't call them Geese) that Ludwigsen flew in Alaska were all US Army Air Corps and US Navy surplus planes. Bob Ellis had flown amphibians such as the Goose, the PBY and the Widgeon during his World War II service and began to buy them up and bring them to Alaska in the late 1940s.

He would eventually have a dozen of the planes, as well a couple of the slightly larger PBYs. Ellis envisioned a region-wide airline that would be capable of carrying large numbers of people and heavy loads but would also be able to land in the water and get into smaller, out of the way destinations.

An amphibian is a little different from a float plane, in that the actual fuselage of the plane becomes a hull for what was essentially a flying boat. It was not sitting on pontoons like a float plane. The Goose could hold up to 11 passengers, roughly twice as many as the largest float planes at the time.

Eventually, the Goose would be adopted by other airlines, including Webber. Ludwigsen said that sometimes they weren't the most efficient to operate and many carriers still used Cessna's and DeHavilland's when they were only picking up a handful of passengers.

The heyday of the Goose in Southeast Alaska effectively ended when the airport for the Ketchikan area was moved from Annette Island (20 miles away from Ketchikan) to Gravina Island (just across Tongass Narrows) and the Goose which were used to shuttle passengers back and forth were replaced by airport ferries to the Gravina Airport.

The shuttle flights themselves always seemed to take some passengers from South by surprise. The passengers had arrived from Seattle in large jets and turboprop airplanes. Then they squeezed into the Grumman's or Consolidated PBYs for the short flight to Ketchikan. Where they landed – much to their surprise – in a big spray of water in front of the town. More than one passenger thought they were crash landing.

Ellis also ran mail runs up and down Southeast Alaska to Craig, Klawock, Wrangell, Petersburg, Sitka, and Juneau.

DeHavilland Beaver

By the early 1970s, the Canadian built DE Havilland Beaver which generally replaced the CESSNA 185 as the workhorse of the Southeast Alaska float plane fleet.

Cessna's were still common, but they had a limited capacity that was not as useful to the air taxi companies.

The Beavers could carry 6 passengers and was also designed for short take-off and landing operations, making them ideal for getting in and out of the region's many lakes. It was powered by a single 450 horsepower Pratt and Whitney engine. It had a cruising speed of 143 mph and a range of 455 miles.

"It was a well-built airplane, real strong, it took a lot of hammering," he said. "It was safe to fly, stable in good and bad air. Easy to load and unload with big doors. It proved to be a very efficient airplane."

Ludwigsen did say there was one flaw with the Beaver's that pilots had to be aware of. If they weren't, it could kill them.

"The Beaver did not have a fuel injection engine like the 185s," he said. "It was a pump that would pump the fuel from the tank forward to the engines carburetor. The outlets on the tanks were on the front part of the tank. It stipulates right in the manual make sure you take off with the best (most full) tank. They didn't explain why, but when you take off with a low fuel tank, it registers on the gauges that you got fuel, but the fuel forces itself to the back of the tank and there's nothing in the lines going to the engine for 10 seconds or sometimes more, depending on how fast you are taking off."

He said more than few pilots have crashed on take-off when the engines stalled in those 10 seconds before the fuel started flowing.

"You're probably about 200 feet in the air," he said. "If you got a heavy (full of passenger or cargo) it won't recover."

He said the Beaver was a generally stable, low flying airplane that packed a much bigger load than the Cessna's and most other float planes.

"It was comfortable to sit in," he said. "I enjoyed sitting in the seats up front. You could do a lot with it, short field landings and lakes. Real safe on that stuff."

He said passengers liked the seats and the large windows for sightseeing.

Ludwigsen said he flew many more hours in a Beaver than in the Grummans because there were many shorter, lower passenger runs to be made in those days.

"It wouldn't pay off in the Grumman," he said. "So, you don't use the big plane."

His favorite Beaver was one that he flew for many years with Southeast Stevedoring. The same Beaver is now flying for Misty Fjords Outfitters and is more than half a century old. Many of the Beavers still in the Southeast Air Taxi fleet are decades old, Ludwigsen said, because newer planes have not been built that are as good.

Cessna's

T-50

Ludwigsen flew several out of the Bethel, calling them the "Grandad of airplanes" with two 300 horsepower Lycoming engines. The T-50s had been developed prior to World War II as twin-engine training planes for bomber pilots.

"They were fine," he said. "I had a lot of fun with them. We took them into some pretty tough places. I liked them. They carried a good load, seven people. We had to use older runways and blacktop runways. Had them on floats, skis or wheels."

"When you had them on skis," he added. "They had a big placard in the cockpit. DON'T RETRACT THE GEAR."

He said he got a lot of twin-engine time flying the T-50s from Bethel out to villages along the Bering Sea coast.

He said he often flew pilots who visited the King Salmon fishing lodges like Kulik or Brooks in the Valley of the Ten Thousand Smokes near Katmai Volcano which had erupted in 1912.

"French pilots, Japanese pilots, one's who flew 747s," he said. "They thought I was crazy. That shaky old airplane, you know. They couldn't believe that thing was still flying."

NUMBER 172

"When I came down from Bethel in 1965, the only airplane Webber let me fly was a Cessna 172," he said. "It was a very underpowered airplane, everybody called it the dog. It was a 260 (hp) engine. "

180

Eventually, Ludwigsen said, he began flying the slightly larger 180.

"It was quite a bit lighter than the 185s," he said. "It was a super plane, like flying a little fighter plane. Lightweight but fairly stable, carried a few passengers. You couldn't get an overload out of it, but she'd fly."

He said the 180 was definitely an upgrade from the 172. "The one I liked the best was the 180," he said. "It didn't have the belly pod and you couldn't overload it. It was a high performing little thing when it was light. Easy to fly. Nothing fancy about it."

He then gave it high praise.

"The 180 was like flying a Super Cub," he said. "It performed well when you knew what to do with it."

185

"The 185 was a fast, fiery little guy," he said. "With a 300-horse engine. She was a good airplane but not built for heavy weather. She wasn't light. She was a fair-weather airplane with floats, you had to be careful, but she could do wonders."

The 185 had more airspeed than a Beaver, but it lacked the short take-off and landing function that the Beaver had, therefore even though it was a peppier plane, with a nearly 140 mph cruising speed, it was not as useful getting into and out of tight spots, Ludwigsen said.

He said the Pratt and Whitney engines in the Beavers and Goose were just more powerful and more reliable than the Continental powerplants in the 185. He also said that the belly pod in the 185 would add 300 pounds more in weight, making the plane more sluggish than the 180.

Piper Super Cub

"The Super Cub was super," he said. "It was crazy, I used it for wolf trapping, taking the family trout fishing. It can't carry much. It's light on the weight."

He said the Webber Piper Super Cub was the airplane that everyone at Webber wanted to use in their free time.

"It's just a well-performing little lightweight airplane," he said. "That was the day-off airplane, you would have to stand in line to get it, there were always a bunch of pilots who wanted to go somewhere. In most pilots' minds, it's the funniest thing to fly."

He said the simplicity of the Super Cub was always a joy.
"You get ready to fly, you pour the power to it and all of a sudden you're flying," he said.

He did note that the small cockpit on the Super Cub was always a little uncomfortable, especially for someone who was 6' 3" like Ludwigsen.

The biggest difference between the Super Cub and most other modern planes is that it had a control stick, rather than a wheel.

"The stick was between your legs, the old standard," he said. "Everyone was happy that Webber Air bought one so the pilots could use it.

Pilatus Porter

When he was flying out of Bethel, he often flew in a Swiss aircraft, the Pilatus Porter. He was not thrilled with the airplane.

"It was a high performing airplane, it was built for the Alps, for skiers," he said. "Had big doors on each side. But it was a very lightweight, flimsy airplane. Had a lot of problems with it. The engine - a 300 hp engine - was terrible. Always blowing cylinders and pilots having a hell of a time trying to make trips with it."

He said, the longer one flew, the cooler the engine got the fewer problems surfaced. The Porter was also a stick and not a wheel.

He said that the nose was extended on most of the Porters and that sometimes led to trouble when a bumpy landing – or sometimes a normal one - could cause the weakly constructed cowling to collapse.

"In the air it flew fine," he said. "It was easy to handle, but nobody really liked to fly them. Still, if you could get it into the air, it was like a little Super Cub."

He said the Porter was well suited for glacier landings and flying in the high altitudes of the Alps, but it was not suited for landings in the Alaska bush where runways were often bumpy, and the plane could occasionally rattle itself apart. He said there were attempts to put the Porters on floats and that was "worse yet."

Curtiss C-46

During his time with Wien Air, Ludwigsen ended up flying the large twin-engine Curtiss-Wright C-46's which had been military cargo planes similar to the DC - 3.

He said the C-46's were "scarier than hell" for him to fly.

"I just wasn't that type of a pilot," he said. "Just fresh out of instrument (school) less than a month. In multi-engine planes I had about four- or five-hours flying time."

He had expected to be a bush pilot and here he was in large cargo planes with twin Pratt and Whitney engines, both pumping out 2,000 horsepower.

"I'm a ground contact pilot," he said. "I don't believe in getting up above the clouds where you can lose your cool and can't get down."

He said he flew 250 hours in the C-46s in everyday runs between Fairbanks and the North Slope.

"The airplanes handled fine," he said. "And the pilots let me fly the left seat, they wanted me to know what the hell I was doing, especially with the radio contacts and directions. I could fly it easy. I had to; it was a job."

Often, the C-46 were flying up to seven tons of cargo between Fairbanks and the Distant Early Warning (DEW) radar sites that were being built along the coast. "It was just the idea that we were flying awfully heavy loads," he said. "I'd look back at heavy steel and tons of stuff back there, just tied with little restraints." He said he knew that if the plane had trouble landing, that heavy cargo would run over the crew immediately.

It didn't help that he was having to get to the airport at 3AM for early morning flights in either the endless daylight or the endless dark above the Arctic Circle.

He did say that sometimes, they would chase polar bears on the sea ice with the large planes.

Herman Ludwigsen Finds Plane Wreckage At Boca de Quadra; Believed Hall Dove

KETCHIKAN Alaska CHRONICLE

Wreckage Hall Dove

EXTRA!

The missing Ellis Hall Dehavilland Dove plane was apparently sighted at Boca de Quadra, about 35 miles each of Ketchikan, at 2 p. m. today by Herman Ludwigsen, Ketchikan amateur flyer, in his Piper two-place plane. If he verifies his find on foot later this afternoon, he will probably claim the $30,000 reward posted by Condor Petroleum company of Texas for finding wreckage of the two-motored plane, lost four weeks ago last night after it left Annette island on a flight to Smithers, B. C.

Ludwigsen came back to Ketchikan, told Webber Air Service from which he and several other flyers were continuing the search, then went back in Dick Jackson's larger, faster plane to inspect the wreckage. They planned to climb to the 2000-foot elevation and see what the timber hid from their view above.

Ludwigsen, who found the wreckage of Fisherman Don Bilderback's plane at Karta lake two weeks ago tomorrow, was flying for C. M. Ashby of Condor Oil, who yesterday renewed the reward offer. Ashby and Pete Cessnun flew over the spot this afternoon to see whether they could verify Ludwigsen's findings.

The Coast Guard also sent a Grumman from Annette at 2:30 this afternoon.

The discovery is not far from where the plane of Harold Gillam of Morrison-Knudsen company crashed in February, 1943, while coming in to Annette from Seattle.

Ludwigsen said he saw what looked like bits of green metal scattered around on the slopes of a timbered area. There were no signs of life or of bodies.

It was recalled that several fish trap watchmen and fishermen saw the Dove plane in Boca de Quadra the night it disappeared, but many others reported seeing it flying back toward Annette airport, which it never reached.

On the plane was wealthy oilman Ellis Hall, his wife, daughters, Joan, 20, and Betty 21, and Patrick Hibben, 17, son of a University of New Mexico professor. Dr. Hibben stayed here for the search for two weeks as did a brother of Hall.

Ludwigsen with Officials

Officials with pilots who helped in locating the wreckage

Pilots Dinner

Former Ketchikan Man Aids Air Force Men Forced Down By Failure of Plane Engine

Search and rescue flights are normal routine in the lives of Alaskan pilots, but a former Ketchikan man probably has spread his attempts to locate or aid downed aircraft over a wider area than most do.

He is Herman Ludwigsen, the son of Mr. and Mrs. Nels Ludwigsen of Ketchikan.

Now operating an aircraft charter service at Bethel, Ludwigsen gained fame here in 1953 when he located a crashed plane at Porpoise point, in Boca de Quadra, which had been object of intensive search for a month.

The DeHavilland Dove carried New Mexico oil executive Ellis Hall, his wife, two daughters, and a 17-year-old youth, Patrick Hibben, to their deaths.

Ludwigsen collected, and shared with nine other Ketchikan pilots who also were searching, $30,000 reward from the Condor Oil company. With his share, Ludwigsen bolstered several local charities, and donated $1000 to build the Little league fieldhouse at Ketchikan ball park.

Bethel Flier

11 RESCUED

A few weeks ago, Ludwigsen rated headlines in Anchorage for his rescue of 11 persons aboard a C123 which crashed on a frozen river bed near Bethel. The air force instructor pilot was able to bring the disabled plane down without injury to anyone aboard. He had broadcast a Mayday signal when one engine failed, Ludwigsen heard the call, and was beside the C123 within 20 minutes.

Personnel of the air force base at Bethel honored the rescue pilot at a dinner. In a letter to his parents here, Ludwigsen indicates that making a speech at the dinner was a tougher assignment than the rescue flight had been.

The former Ketchikan man said he expects to fly at Fort Yukon and Circle city for an oil company during the summer, leaving his wife, Anita, to operate the Bethel charter service with the aid of an Eskimo pilot.

Herman Ludwigsen, son of Mr. and Mrs. Nels Ludwigsen of Ketchikan, was honored by Bethel air force personnel for his assistance to 11 men aboard a plane forced down in a river bed.

BUSH PILOTS HONORED — Bethel bush pilots, from left, Gil Hodgins, Jack Smeaton, Joe Vanderpool and Herman Ludwigson, chat with Col. Jack A. Gibbs, commander of the 10th Air Division; Dr. Harriet Jackson, mayor of Bethel, and Mayor George Byer of Anchorage. The pilots were guests of honor at a dinner given by the 713th Aircraft Control and Warning Squadron at Bethel. The bush pilots rescued the crew of an Elmendorf C123 cargo plane from a frozen river bed 65 miles west of Bethel on Jan. 23, 1960. The C123 Provider has since been repaired and returned to Elmendorf. (Air Force Photo)

Herman's Parents Nels and Amalie Ludwigsen

Ann's Parent's Max and Sophie Lieb

Herman Fishing in the early 1940's

At Webbers mid-1940's

Late 1940's

Amalie

Shooting Hoops
KETCHIKAN ROCKETS—1948

Back, left to right:
Johnny Mills
Lars Farstad
Herman Ladwigen
Bill Christiansen
Joe Boldus
Art Olson

Front, left to right:
Harry Ladwigen
Larry Erickson
Bert Doucette

Ketchikan Rockets - Hall of Fame 1961
1st Gold Medal recipients

112

In the Army

In the Army ... continued

2nd Scout Battalion - Bethel

2nd Scout Battalion at Yukon River

In the Army ... continued

Cessna 195 at Hanger Lake

Tundra Shack with Ann

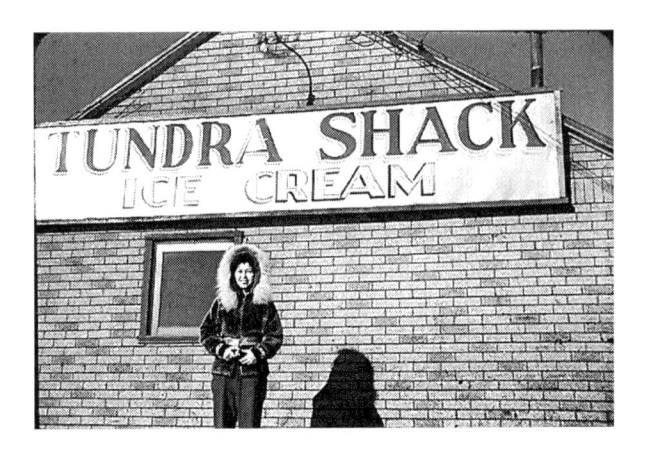

Herman and Ann's Wedding

Herman and Ann

Honeymoon in Hong Kong

PAN AM Tamgas Mountain Crash Site

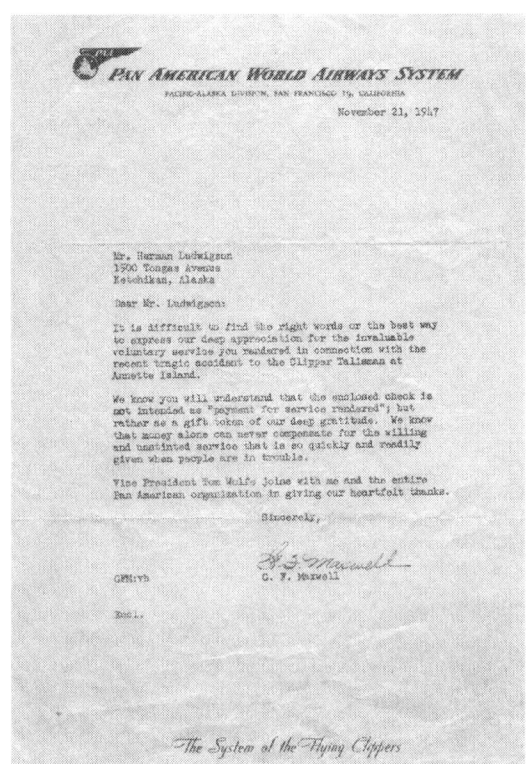

PAN AMERICAN WORLD AIRWAYS SYSTEM
PACIFIC-ALASKA DIVISION, SAN FRANCISCO 19, CALIFORNIA

November 21, 1947

Mr. Herman Ludwigsen
1900 Tongass Avenue
Ketchikan, Alaska

Dear Mr. Ludwigsen:

It is difficult to find the right words or the best way to express our deep appreciation for the invaluable voluntary service you rendered in connection with the recent tragic accident to the Clipper Talisman at Annette Island.

We know you will understand that the enclosed check is not intended as "payment for service rendered"; but rather as a gift token of our deep gratitude. We know that money alone can never compensate for the willing and unstinted service that is so quickly and readily given when people are in trouble.

Vice President Tom Wolfe joins with me and the entire Pan American organization in giving our heartfelt thanks.

Sincerely,

C. F. Maxwell

GFM:yb

Encl.

The System of the Flying Clippers

Bethel Charter Service

Plane on skis

Nelson Island with school in background

Plane on platoons

Bethel Charter Service .... continued

On Kilbuck Mountain

Frozen River broken Gear

Bethel Charter Service .... continued

Frozen River Landing Gear broken

Charter with Neil Smith

Shell Oil Camp

Mountain Point Landing 1953

Lands Plane On Tongass Highway

When Herman Ludwigsen landed his 3-place Piper Cruiser plane at Mountain Point yesterday, he was not instituting a new mail-passenger service to that burgeoning community.

Instead, he had been forced to move the wheel plane from its hangar at Annette. So members of his family halted traffic and he landed it on a straight stretch of the road, without incident. Then its wings were taken off and it was brought to town for storage until he can build a hangar for it and install pontoons.

Ludwigsen, a Kayhi graduate, acquired the plane while in the army and flew it back from Bethel a few weeks ago.

Shell Oil Camp

In the town of Umiat

Downtown Umiat

Shell Oil Camp …. Continued

Porcupine River north of Fort Yukon Village 1950's

Pilatus Porter
Northern Consolidated Airlines (NCA)

Stuck in snow at Flat Old Mining

NCA Plane on platoons

NCA .... Continued

Family Picnic

Mail Run

More NCA ....

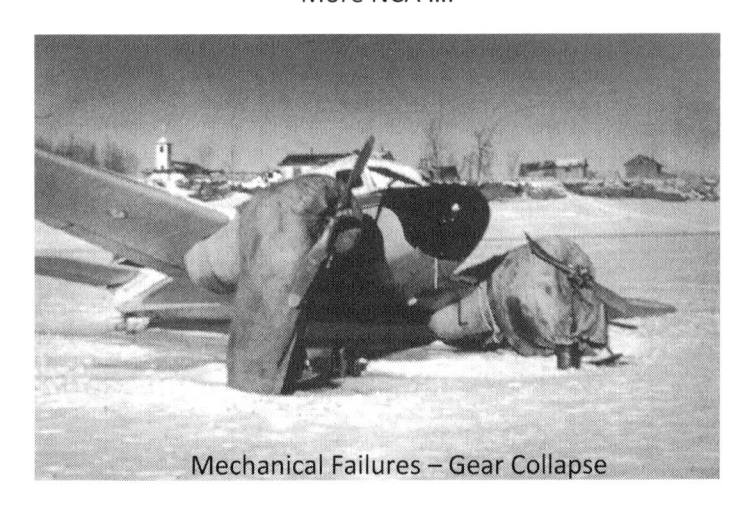

Mechanical Failures – Gear Collapse

Repairing Landing Gear

C123 Accident Mid-1950's

Herman's Plane between the two C-123's

Downdraft Lake Crash

FAA Inspector investigating crash

Webber Air Airplanes

Grumman Goose

Working for Webber Airlines

Webber Pilots (1975)
Jim McDonald, Chuck Slagle, Dave Richie, Jack Swaim,
Herman Ludwigsen and Lynn Campbell

Coast Guard Crash

Fatal Crash

Halibut on Pontoons

Trolling for Salmon

Successful Wolf Hunt

Wolf and Deer on Pontoons

Loading Otters **Loading Otters**

Ready to go to new home

Unloading  Free to go!

Herman in the 1960's

In the Cockpit

More Herman…….

At Iscoot River

At Ketchikan Dock

Ann at Ketchikan Dock

Old and Bold Alaskan Pilots
Kenny Eicker, Don Ross and Herman Ludwigsen

Herman and Terry Wills

Grandson Max and Pop Pop

Max Following in Pop Pops Footsteps

Master Pilot Award

FEDERAL AVIATION ADMINISTRATION

CERTIFICATE OF TRUE COPY

I HEREBY CERTIFY that the attached is a true copy of the complete airman file pertaining to Herman Nels Jorgensen, date of birth November 20, 1927. Supporting documents are on file in the Airmen Certification Branch, Federal Aviation Administration, Department of Transportation.

Signed and dated at Oklahoma City, Oklahoma
this 11th day of March, 2020

Tammie Silk
by Tammie Silk
Compliance Specialist, Airmen Certification Branch
(Title)

I HEREBY CERTIFY that I, Robin M. Thurman, is now and was at the time of signing, Manager, Airmen Certification Branch, Federal Aviation Administration, Department of Transportation, the legal custodian of the aforesaid records, and that full faith and credit should be given this certificate as such.

IN WITNESS WHEREOF, I have hereunto subscribed my name and caused the seal of the U.S. Department of Transportation to be affixed
this 11th day of March, 2020
at Oklahoma City, Oklahoma

Robin M. Thurman
Robin M. Thurman
(Signature)
Manager, Airmen Certification Branch
(Title)
Civil Aviation Registry
U.S. Department of Transportation

The Wright Brothers Master Pilot Award

presented to

Herman Nels Ludwigsen

In recognition of your 50 years of exemplary aviation flight experience, distinguished professionalism, and steadfast commitment to aviation safety.

Steve Dickson, FAA Administrator

June 2020

January 27, 2020

Federal Aviation Administration
Juneau FSDO
Juneau, Alaska

Attn: FSDO Manager or FAASTeam Program Manager

RE: Herman Ludwigsen

To Whom it May Concern:

I have known Herman Ludwigsen since 1972 when I first came to Ketchikan, Alaska and started my aviation career. It is without hesitation that I highly recommend him for the Wright Brothers Master Pilot Award.

I have worked with well over a hundred pilots during my long aviation career in Ketchikan and without exception we all look to Herman Ludwigsen as the example we want to follow. He not only operated his own assigned aircraft in a safe and professional manner at all times, but he was always encouraging the rest of us to do the same. It was not unusual for him to take me or one of the other pilots aside and talk to us about something of concern he saw in our flying habits or skills.

Herman is a man of good moral character. He is an outstanding individual who has had a long and successful career in flying, training, and influencing other pilots. He mentored many young pilots with an ongoing emphasis on safety and longevity. He is respected and is a legend in the Ketchikan Aviation Community.

My knowledge and association with Herman spans my entire flying career in Ketchikan, Alaska. He has been a fabulous example and mentor to me and many, many other pilots who have flown in Ketchikan and throughout Alaska.

I have held pilot certificate 2171695 since 1972.

Respectfully Submitted,

Kirk M. Thomas
104 Mountain Ash Heights, Ketchikan, Alaska 99901
kirkt@aseresorts.com / (907) 821-6833

Master Pilot Letter of recommendation

LISA MURKOWSKI
ALASKA

United States Senate
WASHINGTON, D.C. 20510

September 25, 2020

Mr. Herman Ludwigsen
4640 North Tongass Highway, Apartment 104
Ketchikan, AK 99901

Dear Herman,

Congratulations on receiving the Wright Brothers Master Pilot Award. This is a tremendous accomplishment as you are now recognized as one of Alaska's flight pioneers. Because so many of our communities are remote, Alaskans depend on the brave men and women of our aviation industry, like you, for lifesaving services, supplies and transportation.

Your contributions are one of the many reasons Alaska is such a wonderful place to live and raise a family. Thank you for the contributions that you have made to Alaska's development and the aviation community.

Sincerely,

Lisa Murkowski
United States Senator

I miss seeing you on our trips into Prince of Wales! My best

NOT PRINTED AT TAXPAYER EXPENSE

Master Pilot Award Congratulations from Senator Lisa Murkowski

Representative Dan Ortiz

Alaska State Legislature / Ketchikan, Saxman, Wrangell, Hydaburg, Metlakatla, Hyder, Loring and Meyers Chuck

SESSION ADDRESS:
Alaska State Capitol
Juneau, Alaska 99801
Phone: 907-465-3824
Toll Free: 1-800-686-3824
Fax: 907-465-3175

INTERIM ADDRESS:
1900 First Avenue, Suite 310
Ketchikan, Alaska 99901
Phone: 907-247-4672
907-465-5269
Fax: 907-225-8546

Herman Ludwigsen
4640 N Tongass Hwy, Apt 104
Ketchikan, AK 99901

October 7, 2020

Herman,

Congratulations on being awarded the Federal Aviation Administration's Wright Brothers Master Pilot Award! As the most prestigious FAA award, it honors your undeniable professionalism, skill, and aviation expertise for over a half of a century.

I am impressed by your piloting statistics, with over 50 years and 32,000 hours of experience flying in Alaska. Even more so, I am impressed by your dedication and integrity. Thank you for using your skills, including your 'sixth sense,' to help locate multiple downed airplanes. Those recoveries have helped bring peace and closure to so many friend and families of pilots and passengers.

While reading the Ketchikan Daily News Article, I enjoyed learning about your life, from your years at Ketchikan High School to your years in Bethel. We are lucky here in Southeast that you chose to make Ketchikan your primary home. You have been an asset to our community, especially our flying community. Once again, thank you for your years as a pilot and congratulations on being awarded such a prestigious and well-earned honor.

Respectfully,

Representative Dan Ortiz

Master Pilot Award Congratulations from Rep. Dan Ortiz

DAN SULLIVAN
ALASKA

UNITED STATES SENATE
WASHINGTON, D.C. 20510

September 28, 2020

Mr. Herman N. Ludwigsen
4640 North Tongass Highway, Apartment 104
Ketchikan, AK 99901-9052

Dear Herman,

It is my pleasure to congratulate you on receiving the prestigious Federal Aviation Administration *Wright Brothers Master Pilot Award*.

During your over 50 years of flying your friends and neighbors around Southeast Alaska, you have demonstrated a selfless commitment to aviation safety and been a positive role model for aspiring pilots. Thank you for your dedication to the State of Alaska, and aviation in particular.

Again, I extend my congratulations and most sincere appreciation for your many years of service.

Sincerely,

Dan Sullivan
United States Senator

Congrats again Herman!
- Dan

Master Pilot Award Congratulations from Senator Dan Sullivan

Alaska Coastwise Pilots Association
P.O. Box 23367
Ketchikan, Alaska 99901-8367

Marine Pilotage
Dispatch Service

Telephone: (907) 225-7245
Fax: (907) 247-4568

September 4, 1998

Herman Ludwigsen
Southeast Stevedoring Corporation
P.O. Box 8080
Ketchikan, AK 99901

Dear Herman,

We, at ACPA, would like to congratulate you on your retirement. Your 52 years of safe flying in Alaska prove the old saying that there are no "old, bold pilots".

We would like you to know that we have appreciated your expertise and calm, wise judgement on numerous safe flights that we have taken under your care. We will miss you (in fact, there are some among us who fear flying with anyone else).

However, we do recognize, that this retirement was hard earned and we wish you well in your new endeavors in Wrangell. We hope you will drop in occasionally when you're in town. Happy gardening!

Sincerely,

Captain Joseph W Homer
President

Captain Jeff Baken
Secretary/Treasurer

Kelly Jenks
Office Manager

Retirement Letter

January 25, 2020

To Whom It May Concern:

It is a pleasure to have the opportunity to write about one of my true heroes, Herman Ludwigsen. Herman was a presence in my life from an early age. I first met Herman in 1970, when I was a freshman in high school. I would work at Webber Air after school where Herman was the chief pilot. It was my job to load the airplanes and fuel them. Herman had an instinct and knowledge of flying in Alaska that was a rare gift. If anyone had a question or needed guidance, he was there to help. I was a young pilot "wannabe" with no ratings or licenses. Herman looked out for me and helped me to start my journey in aviation.

Herman was respected at Webber Air and throughout the Southeast Alaska aviation community. He made a practice of taking the flights when the weather was marginal or the destination difficult. He knew the airplane and the Southeast area so well that he was truly the best pilot for these flights. He would also make sure to fly with all the less experienced pilots to teach them the "ins and outs" of flying in this unforgiving area of Alaska. He had a knack of helping you to learn not just so you could be a better pilot but to keep you alive! All of us young pilots watched Herman, flew with him, and listened to his advice.

After college I was determined to make aviation my career. Herman definitely inspired that desire. The knowledge that Herman had instilled during all those years when I was a dock boy stayed with me. Every step of the way he was encouraging. Eventually, I would leave floatplane flying and have a 30-year career at Alaska Airlines flying jets. During my career at Alaska Airlines I came in contact with a number of other pilots that credited Herman with teaching them important flying lessons. I feel very fortunate to have benefited from the friendship with Herman that always had its teachable moments. I made most of my worst floatplane landings in front of the Webber Air dock and every time I parked the airplane Herman was either walking down the ramp to talk to me or waiting at the top of the ramp to discuss the landing. There was a lesson in each landing and Herman was the best pilot to critique your performance.

As a young pilot learning the ropes of flying, Herman was a larger than life figure. Without his guidance and wisdom, I would not have had the success in my own aviation career. He was my guardian angel in my early years and a constant presence always. Writing this letter of recommendation is an honor.

Herman is an aviation legend in Alaska. I cannot think of a better aviator to receive this prestigious award.

Sincerely,

Michael J. Cessnun

Michael J. Cessnun

Alaska Airlines Pilot, Retired

Character Reference Letter

01/27/2020

Juneau FSDO

Attn: Lana Boier

I have known Herman Ludwigsen since 1975. I worked with Herman as a dock boy. He trained me to fly and was my mentor for many years. I credit Herman with helping me to be an excellent pilot.

Herman is a legend in Ketchikan, AK. He was instrumental in all aspects of the aviation community in Ketchikan. Herman was the man that everyone wanted to work with, be trained by and to emulate.

Herman was always a safe and professional pilot. I highly recommend him for the Wright Brothers Master Pilot Reward. I cannot think of anyone more deserving.

I hold Pilot Certificate number 574224905.

Respectfully submitted,

Jeff Carlin

Jeff Carlin Digitally signed by Jeff Carlin
Date: 2020.03.06 09:08:19 -09'00'

Carlin Air

1249 Tongass Ave.

Ketchikan, AK 99901

hef@kpunet.net

(907) 617-3482

Character Reference Letter

Form ACA 301
(Rev. 8-48)

UNITED STATES OF AMERICA
DEPARTMENT OF COMMERCE
CIVIL AERONAUTICS ADMINISTRATION
WASHINGTON

School Graduation Certificate

This is to certify that **Herman Nels Ludwigsen** (Name)

Route 1 Box 412, Ketchikan, Alaska (Address) was graduated from the

Multi-Engine Land and Sea curriculum of the

Renton Aviation, Inc. (School)

Renton Municipal Airport, Renton, Wn. (Address) Airman Agency Certificate No. **60123**

on **June 5, 1956** (Date); that he has successfully completed the instruction required by the Civil Air Regulations and is eligible to apply for a **Commercial Pilot** Certificate and **AMEL & AMES** Rating as issued by the Administrator of Civil Aeronautics.

The record of this graduate is as follows:

Flying time:

Dual ___ 7:40 ___

Solo ___

Total ___ 7:40 ___

Final flying grade ___ 84% ___

COURSES SATISFACTORILY COMPLETED   GRADE

I certify that the above statements are true.

RENTON AVIATION, INC.
(School)

By _____ (Signature)

President (Title)

Date issued **6/5/56**

Certificate to operate Multi-engine Land and Sea Craft

Certificate of Accomplishment

PRESENTED BY

FLYING TIGERS

This is to certify that

Herman Ludwigsen

has participated in and successfully completed
a Flying Tigers Hazardous Materials Seminar.

By participation in this program,
the above-named individual has demonstrated a dedication to the
development and growth of the airfreight industry.

Director-Safety

June 27, 1980
Date

THE CONFEDERATE AIR CORPS

To all who shall see these presents, greeting:

Know ye, that in recognition of his having manifested an unusually high regard for black-eyed peas, turnip greens, hog jowl, sow belly, pot likker, grits, chittlins, and good old corn squeezins,

Herman N. Ludwigsen

is as of this date hereby appointed to the rank of **Colonel** in the

Confederate Air Corps

This officer will, by virtue of this appointment, therefore, be obliged to carefully and diligently discharge the duties of the office to which appointed by doing and performing all manner of things thereunto belonging.

As evidence of his good faith in accepting this commission, the officer named herein will continue to praise the glories of the Deep South, consume a true gentleman's share of the fare mentioned above, pay respectful homage to our lovely Southern Belles, save her Confederate money, harass the carpetbaggers, and always remember that damnyankee is one word.

As Secretary of this Corps, I strictly charge and require all officers of this air militia of the South to render such obeisance and courtesies as are due an Officer of this distinguished rank and honored position.

Done at the City of Montgomery, Alabama, The Cradle of the Confederacy, this **Twenty-sixth** day of **January** in the year One Thousand Nine Hundred and Fifty **Nine**.

Thadius P. Throckmorton
Secretary
Confederate Air Corps

Santa Barbara Savings

FRANK M. CONSOLE *Executive Vice President*   Santa Barbara Savings and Loan Association P.O. Drawer D-D Santa Barbara, California 93102

August 27, 1969

Dear Herman:

I have been meaning to get a thank you note off to you for the last week but have been too busy playing catch-up here in the office since returning from Alaska. I also wanted to tell you that I am sorry we couldn't get together for dinner before leaving Ketchikan.

We had a great trip up the inland channel up to Skagway and then back to Juneau. Flew home from Juneau and through it all only lost one piece of luggage on Alaska Airlines (still haven't found it).

Since returning, I have had many laughs telling my friends about the great deer hunt with Herman and how I kept falling down the hillside and missing good shots. Seriously, that was by far the most enjoyable hunt I have ever had. As tired as I got, I would do it again any time just to see all of those deer and the beautiful country. It was also kind of exciting taking off in the supercub from that small lake.

Anyway, I want to thank you for making it all possible and to let you know that if I can ever do anything for you when you are down this way, just let me know and it will be taken care of.

Say hello to Pete and the others at Webber Air. We hope to see you all again in a year or so.

Best regards,

Frank

Thank you letter from Executive Vice President of Santa Barbara Savings

ERNEST F. HOLLINGS
SOUTH CAROLINA

United States Senate
WASHINGTON, D.C. 20510

October 15, 1971

Dear Herman:

I don't know when I've had a thrill to equal seeing the magnificent glaciers in Alaska. It was truly one of the most beautiful sights Peatsy and I have ever seen -- and it was due to you that we were able to see it.

Many thanks and I hope you will call on me if you get to Washington.

Sincerely,

Fritz.

Mr. Herman Ludwigson
Box 761
Ketchikan, Alaska 99901

Thank you letter from the office of Senator Hollings of South Carolina

TED STEVENS

October 14, 1971

Dear Herman:

It was good to see you last week.

I want to thank you for all you did to make the trip pleasant for Senator and Mrs. Hollings. I thought everything was great, and I have heard Senator Hollings has been telling quite a few members of the Senate about the trip. Alaska must have made quite an impression.

Thanks again for all you did.

With best wishes,

Cordially,

TED STEVENS
United States Senator

Mr. Herman Ludwigsen
P. O. Box 761
Ketchikan, Alaska 99901

Thank you letter from Senator Ted Stevens

FRANK H. MURKOWSKI
ALASKA

United States Senate
WASHINGTON, D.C.

November 19, 1985

Mr. Herman Ludwigsen
2526 Fourth
Ketchikan, Alaska 99901

Dear Herman:

I just wanted you to know how much Nancy and I and my staff enjoyed the flights from Petersburg to Wrangell and Ketchikan. The weather was good, but the pilot was excellent.

Flying over the Narrows is always a great treat for me.

Many thanks, Herman.

Sincerely,

Frank H. Murkowski
United States Senator

No more Ducks - but Gel hope you get a Deer!

Thank you letter from Senator Frank Murkowski

JOHN A. DURKIN
NEW HAMPSHIRE

COMMITTEES:
ENERGY AND NATURAL
RESOURCES
COMMERCE, SCIENCE AND
TRANSPORTATION
VETERANS' AFFAIRS

United States Senate
WASHINGTON, D.C. 20510
June 22, 1978

OFFICES:
SENATE OFFICE BUILDING
202-224-3324
WASHINGTON, D.C. 20510
FEDERAL BUILDING
603-431-5900
PORTSMOUTH, NEW HAMPSHIRE 02801
FEDERAL BUILDING
603-666-7681
MANCHESTER, NEW HAMPSHIRE 03101

Mr. Herman Ludwigsen
Webber Airlines
Ketchikan, Alaska 99901

Dear Ludwigsen:

At this time I would like to thank you for your kindness on my recent trip to Alaska. The treatment I received from everyone associated with the visit was particularly heartwarming because of my deep admiration for the State of Alaska and her people.

The Senate will soon be considering the Alaskan land issue and it is of great importance to me in assuring that a comprehensive, equitable Bill emerges from the full Senate.

Having the opportunity to revisit Alaska, served to greatly increase my understanding of the land and appreciation for its people. I am truly looking forward to visiting again in the near future and renewing our relationship.

With kindest regards,

Sincerely,

John A. Durkin

JAD/mhh

Many thanks for everything

TOLL FREE CITIZEN HOT LINE
(800) 562-1110

Thank you letter from Senator John Durkin, New Hampshire

ORDER OF THE
ALASKA WALRUS

LET IT BE KNOWN that during the year 196 7

Herman Ludwigsen

did visit Alaska, the largest State of the United States.

LET IT BE KNOWN, too, that while visiting Alaska this Visitor did experience the beauty of Alaska's scenic grandeur, the thrill of her vast wilderness, and the warmth not only of her climate but of her people as well.

LET IT BE KNOWN, therefore, that because this Visitor is thus qualified, I have set my name and seal to this document and proclaim said Visitor to be a lifetime member in good standing of the:

ORDER OF THE ALASKA WALRUS

Done at Juneau, the Capital of Alaska.

Walter J. Hickel
Governor of Alaska and the
Walrus' Domain

Witness:

Yukon-Kuskokwim Health Corporation
1-800-478-2905
"Fostering Native Self-Determination in Primary Care, Prevention and Health Promotion"

May 14, 1992

Mr. Herman Ludwigsen
Box 679
Ward Cove, Alaska 99928

Dear Mr. Ludwigsen:

Each year the Yukon Kuskokwim Health Corporation holds an awards banquet to honor the hard working employees and departments from the previous year. This year we added another set of awards that we felt were long overdue.

YKHC wanted to thank the wonderful, dedicated pilots who, flying through rain, sleet and snow, unselfishly served to ensure the safe transport of the people of the YK Delta. While risking much you have saved many and upheld the YKHC Corporate Mission.

The enclosed plaque is a very small token of our appreciation and gratitude.

Quyana.

Sincerely,

Gene Peltola
President/CEO

cc: Awards Banquet File

P.O. Box 528   Bethel, Alaska 99559   Phone: (907) 543-3321   Fax: (907) 543-5277

Awards Dinner invitation

THE OFFICE OF SARAH PALIN

Very Nice

Todd and I want to thank you for your thoughtful gift. The overwhelming number of cards, gifts, poems and words of support we receive reminds us daily how blessed we are with the opportunities we have been given.

Your kindness is truly appreciated and I thank you for your continued support for me and my family and your interest in the future of our great country.

God Bless You,

Sarah Palin

ALASKA
P.O. Box 871235
WASILLA, AK 99687

VIRGINIA
P.O. Box 7711
ARLINGTON, VA 22207

Paid for by SarahPAC

August 23, 2001 WRANGELL SENTINEL - Page 7

Former pilot gets grounded in gardening

By Bonnie Demerjian
Sentinel staff writer

Herman Ludwigsen called the Sentinel to boast about his begonias, and we're glad he did. We made a trip out Zimovia Highway to see his flowers and were stunned to see not only mammoth displays of begonias, but six-foot Asian lilies, raspberry bushes laden with fruit and many other plants, some of them unusual transplants to Southeast Alaska.

Herman and his wife Anita moved to Wrangell two and a half years ago from Ketchikan to be with their son, Manny, and his family. Ludwigsen is a retired pilot for Southeast Stevedoring who has taken up gardening with enthusiasm and energy after forty-six years of flying. He began to take an interest in the subject while still a pilot, however. He made frequent trips to Prince Rupert and, while there, began buying plants to bring back to Ketchikan. Pink-flowered Yukon strawberries which are extra hardy, are one of his successful transplants. Another unusual plant which he first tried in Ketchikan, then brought to Wrangell, is the fragrant Balm of Gilead tree, a close relation to the familiar black cottonwood found up the Stikine.

Ludwigsen says his begonias, including one giant bulb which fills a pot on its own, were all purchased in Canada. Each fall, after the foliage dies back, he takes the bulbs from the soil, spreads them in boxes to dry, and overwinters them in his greenhouse. There they stay until early February when he places them in soil-filled pots and keeps them in the greenhouse until the last frost. He says this year he had to carry them in and out doors several times before the weather settled into spring. A basement is also a fine place for keeping the bulbs in soil as long as it's not too hot or cold. During the growing season, he uses a 20-20-20 fertilizer mixed with water.

His Wrangell garden features one of his favorite plants - raspberries. Ludwigsen's garden has four varieties including the less familiar golden yellow and purple ones. Pansies spill out of a handcrafted yellow cedar planter. The planter is his own design and he has made several in varying sizes which he is planning to market to Wrangell gardeners.

We're glad that Wrangell gardeners aren't shrinking violets. They work hard and achieve truly impressive results, so why not brag a little?

Photo by Bonnie Demerjian
Herman Ludwigsen is deservedly proud of his flowers. Here he poses with Asiatic lilies and begonias in hanging planters.

Ludwigsen still gardening

Article in Wrangell Sentinel 2001

HERMAN LUDWIGSEN'S STORY: HOMETOWN BOY MAKES GOOD

A spectacular end to a spectacular airplane search came today and yesterday in Boca de Quadra, the octopus-like "in- land cauldron" which now has claimed the planes of Ellis Hall of Albuquerque and Harold Gillam (Morrison Knud-sen), ten and one-half years before. When this corner set out four weeks ago today to organize the plane search for Condor Petroleum company, we had a feeling in our minds that a light plane flown by a bush pilot would find the missing Dehavilland Dove, if it ever was found. We offered to bet that this would be the case, but found no takers.

Bob Ellis and Pete Cessnun, the actual directors of volunteer search operations, had the same conviction, that light planes in the hands of boys who were not afraid to fly over the tree tops, would uncover the wreckage, if it, ever was to be found.

They had seen Alaska's young men, as we have some years and for had faith in their ability. The same feeling affected C. M. Ashby who came up a week ago to continue the search after the Coast Guard and air force gave up. Gordon Gray went to Smithers and hired five amateurs to comb the area, while Ashby came here. He told his colleagues in Texas that if the plane was found, a light plane flying low would do it. For Cessnun, too, the discovery of the lost plane was a personal triumph.

He taught most of the men who stayed on the plane search to fly since the war. And he went over to Boca de Quadra to look it over before Hermann Ludwigsen was sent out on what proved to be a successful mission. As for young Ludwigsen, the son of a prominent local family, all of them respected members of the community, we think he deserved the publicity he has been accorded and his share of the reward. He will not claim it all for he was a member of the winning team. And the $5000 ear - marked for charity, he will put into several local causes- part of it at our suggestion into a continuing fund for future search and rescue operations. That type of fund could save lives in the future, perhaps of some of our own townspeople. Hermann is a clean, jolly, 'likable young man. He is the better type of product of Alaska. He loves and is at home the outdoors; totally without fear, but full of confidence in himself. He convinced the army that he knows Alaska and Alaskans, so the army sent him out to the western tundra country to help train the native guardsmen, and there he did an outstanding job, learned to fly, and fell in love with a cute little girl who has some Eskimo blood in her veins.

Hermann came home from his army service last winter in his own newly acquired Piper three-place plane. He met his old friends, saw some of his old girl friends, and decided that the girl back in Bethel was as sweet as any. Besides, she didn't smoke or drink. So he sent for her and married her in his old home town. Two weeks ago Hermann found the wreckage of Don Bilderback's plane at Karta lake. Yesterday he was flying over Boca de Quadra where he had made dozens of trips while spotting fish for seineboats. A streak of white went by and he wondered why there would be snow at that altitude in mid-September.

"I turned around and had another look. And boy! I just about jumped out of my plane," he told us last night. That's about all there is to the Ellis Hall plane search, except the details on the front page. We Alaskans just go about our business, despite the inferiority complex caused by our minor status as colonials. And we do the best way we know how. But if there is an Almighty-and every day we see evidence that there is-we are glad that He chose young men like Hermann Ludwigsen to do some of his more important business here below.

It seems quit fit. In fact, it took some of the tragedy off the loss of the Hall family of four and the lively, eager 17-year-old Patrick Hibben.

From The "Daily News" 1953

"A FIELD GUIDE TO WEBBER AIRPILOT SPECIE BIRDS"

--a standard series for field identification--

THIS MONTH: **A HERMLUDWIGSEN**

(Species: OLDTIMER-BUSH PILOT)
Known in Alaskan bird circles as a green backed, receding forehead (or single tufted) long legged Norsebeak.
Often confused with similar species called boat-builder or housebuilder Ludwigsen. Of same family except other Ludwigsens are flightless.
RANGE: 250 to 400 miles from Ketchikan nesting area. In flight, axis of body is virtually horizontal. Always a leader generally carries one to eight paying parasites in flight who promptly leave when grounded.
FIELD MARKS: Sheds body cover to resemble Goose, Beaver or Cessna (sub-specie) dep- ending on necessity.
Flies singly and cautiously in most weather. (Avoids heavy winds or areas of low visibility. Generally sits on dock in adverse weather. Can then be readily identified by cup in claw).
Flies with certainty as if extremely knowledgeable of area. Indeed, the Hermludwigsen is the oldest of Webberairpilot specie. Has been sighted in area for the past many years.
VOICE: Soft spoken, except for low grunts in nesting colony.
WHERE FOUND: All Southeast Alaska - particularly in lakes or rivers occupied by heavy large trout. Also frequents logging camps and villages on Prince of Wales Island.

Occasionally spotted as far north as Yakutat (generally in fall) near moose flats. Winters on hillside in Ketchikan suggesting more than casual status in area.
A VERY FRIENDLY BIRD.

(NEXT MONTH: A ALLENZINK,

Ludwigsen's favorite plane - the Grumman Goose #45

Our dad flew from sunup to sundown in all seasons. When our dad had a day off, he would say "I know I have children because the food keeps disappearing!" As teenagers the last place we wanted to be was stuck at home and hear those dreaded words from dad: "I want to see my children. Cancel what you have going on." As we groaned and complained, we got on the phone to call our friends. Spending time with dad and mom was filled with playing cards (mostly 21) and watching his favorite TV shows or movie.

"I liked mandatory family nights sometimes." Jocelyn recalled. "Because I wanted to finally win a game of 21! I never did."

Lynn Staats
Manny Ludwigsen
Jocelyn Ludwigsen

Moose Camp Breakfast

Jocelyn Ludwigsen

Lynn Staats

Manny Ludwigsen

Made in United States
Troutdale, OR
07/24/2024